An Accidental Love Affair 2

Brittany Desiree'

Published by Shan Presents

www.shanpresents.com

Table of Contents

Chapter 1

Twenty-five years ago…

Dominic "Ace" Malone stood in the lobby of the FBI building in Manhattan, NY. He smiled at the thoughts of finally getting the recognition he deserved. After running point on several successful operations in the last few months, he had gotten the promotion he wanted. He was being moved to Atlanta, GA to work his way up the ranks and get in good with the area's biggest dealer, Damien "Dame" King.

Ace had spent the last two years learning every aspect of the drug game. He was a part of a special FBI team that placed men undercover to infiltrate drug organizations and take down its leaders. In the last two years he had played every position from corner boy to lieutenant. A few months back, while working undercover, he had linked up with a man named Sean who invited him to come to Atlanta and work alongside his boss, Dame.

He had done a full background check on Dame. There were several arrests and open investigations on Damien King. All of them lacked the necessary information needed to take him down. It took nothing for Ace to convince his superiors that he could go down there and bring down a major kingpin. Dame's operation would be the largest he'd ever been a part of, but Ace wasn't afraid.

******

"Daddy…?"

Khloé hadn't seen her father in 12 years. Other than a few grey hairs in his perfectly lined goatee, he didn't look like any time had passed at all. He was still as handsome as she remembered. Dominic Malone stood 6'3 with peanut butter colored skin. He still wore his hair in a low cut style that naturally waved due to the texture of his hair. His almond shaped, brown eyes were hooded beneath thick eyebrows. He had a broad nose, strong jawline, and thick lips. His body was still in good shape as he worked out several times a week. He was dressed casually in dark wash jeans, a black long sleeve Ralph Lauren thermal, and black Timbs.

The two men stepped into her condo, and she closed the door behind them waiting on an explanation. They both walked past her and into the living room where everyone was seated. Not knowing what else to do, Khloé followed. Darren was the first to stand up and greet both men. He was still unaware that Dutch's law connect was actually the twins' father. He shook Ace's hand then pulled Dutch in for a manly hug.

"What's up old nigga?" He greeted his old mentor.

"Kill that old shit. I'll still whoop your little ass." Dutch said laughing. "This is Dominic Malone also known as Ace, Dame's ex-right hand. He's FBI."

Khloé stared at the man who arrived with her father not believing a word Dutch had just said. Her father wasn't a drug dealer nor did he work for the Feds. He had left her family 12 years ago to run off with another woman, right? He was a business man, a lawyer or accountant or something. She ran through all of the different scenarios her and Kai had come up with when they were younger. They'd lay in bed together and come up with reasons why their father abandoned them. When her father didn't say anything, she stormed off to her room, slamming the door. She couldn't believe him.

Elijah and Darren both looked from Khloé to Ace putting two and two together. Somehow Khloé knew this man. The room was silent as everybody was unsure of what to say next.

"I'm her father." Ace said before taking a seat on the sofa.

Darren and Elijah had no idea that the Ace they had heard so many stories about was the twins' father and a dirty agent at that. From Khloé's reaction, they could also tell that she hadn't known either. Elijah came to terms with the newfound revelation easily. He had been wondering how the twins afforded such a lavish lifestyle, and now he had an answer. Darren on the other hand, had fire burning in his hazel eyes as he realized Ace could be the reason his pregnant girlfriend had been kidnapped.

******

Thirteen years ago...

Ace arrived at the warehouse to meet Dame. Everything was set up and he was confident that everything was going to go as planned. He had just got off the phone with Dame's connect a minute ago, and he had assured Ace that everything was good. Ace got out of the car praying that Dame didn't do anything impulsive and ruin his plans. Ace knew that he was taking a chance with his decision. He walked inside with his head up preparing for a faceoff with Dame.

"Mother fucking Agent Dominic Malone. Can't say I saw this shit coming." Dame said giving Ace a slow clap.

Ace tried not to laugh. Dame looked like a big ass gorilla clapping his hands like that. Dame was a big dude. He stood about 6 foot even and about 300 pounds with skin so dark, he was almost black. He had round black eyes, a wide nose, and big lips. His head was shaved bald and shiny.

"So now you got it all figured out, what's your move?" Ace calmly stated. He stood about 4 feet from Dame. He had no fear in his expression or body language.

Dame didn't say a word. He quickly drew his weapon and pointed it at Ace. He went to ask Ace for his final words before he heard about 5 guns click around him. Dame was confused because his men were pointing their guns at him instead of Ace.

The warehouse door opened once more and in walked his connect of the last 5 years. Dame then knew Ace had been successful in taking over his operation. He'd heard rumors, but didn't believe it. Ace always seemed like a stand-up guy. Dame had worked too hard to get to where he was now, he wasn't going down without a fight.

"You mother fuckers working together?" Dame spat angrily.

Ace shook his new connect's hand then exited the warehouse. His job was done. He could now sit back and collect money. He could say that

Dame talked too much and had pretty much given Ace everything he needed to bring him down. Every detail of Dame's operation was thought out carefully and ran like a well-oiled machine. Ace could continue to do his legal job and stack his money on the side without ever having to touch a drug or be in the same room as any. He had already saved up a nice cushion of money he held in an offshore account. Without having to split profit with Dame, he couldn't wait for the money to start piling in.

Ace walked across the parking lot to his brand new Lexus coupe he had just bought last week. He noticed his FBI partner leaning against the door eating an apple.

"Sup, Sam?" Ace shook hands with his partner then opened the driver's side door. He knew Sam showing up here wasn't a good sign, but nothing could prepare him for what news Sam had for him.

"The director said make a choice today. You can go clean and head to the next assignment, or go down with the others." Sam threw down the rest of the apple and walked away without another word.

Ace kicked the wheel of his car and slammed his door shut. He had worked too hard and everything was finally falling in place. He couldn't just walk away now. He had just taken over a multimillion dollar drug operation. The amount of money he would be making would be way more than he made as an agent. He would be able to spend more time with his wife and girls. This was what he had been working so hard for.

On the other hand, he could go down with Dame. He was very careful to walk a fine line while Dame was under investigation, but some of his actions lately could be seen as criminal. He had been taking a lot of meetings with his new plug and hadn't been updating the FBI on any information surrounding him. That alone could send him to prison for a few years. The thought of his girls visiting him in prison and not being able to watch them grow, made his decision easier. He knew what he had to do.

******

Khloé sat leaning against her headboard with her knees pulled up to her chest. She had been feeling like everything that happened to Kai was all her fault because of Blue Wave. Come to find out, Dame and possibly Jesse, had some old grudge against her father. She felt betrayed that Ace, nor her mother, had ever told them what he did for a living. Their parents had hardly been around growing up, so they hadn't had many opportunities to ask a lot of questions. She didn't move when she heard soft knocks on her door and Elijah walked in.

"We about to head out." He let her know so she could come lock the door. He took her key and told her not to open the door for anyone. Khloé nodded that she understood what he was saying. He pulled her in for a hug and she melted into him. Both of them were seriously missing the other, but now wasn't the time for that. Elijah kissed Khloé on the forehead before walking out of her bedroom with her following behind. The guys then filed out of the door to go bring Kai home.

Chapter 2

"You good?" Dutch said pulling Ace from his thoughts and handing him a lit blunt.

"I was supposed to be there. I thought I was doing the right thing in leaving. I still had my job intact and the side money was still flowing in. Those girls had everything they could need and more. I knew O would take good care of them, but she pawned them off on some random nanny as soon as I left.

"The FBI was on my back so hard. Jail or leave Atlanta, I had to make a choice. Look where my choice got me, though. My baby girl is out there pregnant and probably scared. The other one is home crying, and I have no idea what to say or do to comfort her." Ace hit the blunt.

Dutch didn't know what to say so he listened quietly as his old friend let out all of his feelings. Being in Atlanta was bringing out old skeletons for Dutch as well. He knew now wasn't the time to reveal secrets of his own, but they were eating him inside. They needed to focus on bringing back Kai and taking out Dame. Dutch was finally going to offer up some advice when he noticed Elijah and Darren walking up. They had just returned from scoping out the building.

The old cotton mill was a rundown two-story brick building on a deserted street in old Hapeville. It appeared that

Dame had stationed two men to guard the outside. They took turns circling the building in opposite directions. They had radios, which Zane was trying to tap into to see who they were speaking to. Before they proceeded, they needed to know how many men were inside the building. They still had about 30 minutes before the meet time and were feeling confident that they would be bringing Kai home tonight.

After changing the channel a few times on his own radio, Zane finally found the station where Dame's men were talking. They could now hear the men going back and forth laughing and joking. From the voices and amount of laughter in the background, Zane could tell that they were definitely outnumbered by Dame's men. Elijah immediately got on his phone and called up Black, the new leader of his East Point trap house. After telling Black to round up the crew and where to meet, Elijah hung up the phone.

"Let's be smart about this. My woman and my unborn seed are in there." Darren said to everyone as they all checked their weapons and prepared to go in full force. He was hoping they wouldn't have to use any guns at all, but he knew better. You didn't show up to a gunfight with a knife, and they were all well prepared. Elijah got a text from Black saying the crew was about 15 minutes out. He nodded to Darren to let him know that they had backup on the way.

Ace didn't really feel comfortable letting Darren run everything. Ace didn't know what was going on between Darren and his daughter, but he knew that Kai shouldn't have been trying to drive home at almost midnight by herself, being that she was 5 months pregnant. She shouldn't have been driving at all. After this was all over with and his baby girl was back home safely, he would need to have a talk with Darren about protecting his daughter.

Dutch and Darren crept alongside the building and snuck up behind the two guards. The guards were engaged in a friendly conversation and weren't paying attention to anything going on around them as they shared a cigarette between them and laughed. They each hit one of the guards in the back of the head with the butt of their guns knocking them out instantly. Darren took some rope and bound their hands together. They then gave the signal back to the others to follow. They went to the backdoor of the building. Dutch stuck his ear to the door to see if he could hear anyone standing on the other side. His adrenaline was pumping. He hadn't been out in the streets like this in a long time.

BOOM! With one kick, Darren burst through the door. They had caught the men inside by surprise as the front door came crashing down as well. Black and about 15 other men filed into the room with their guns drawn. Dame's men had no choice but to surrender.

"GET DOWN NOW!" Elijah shouted to five of Dame's men who stood in the middle of the large room talking. Seeing that they were outnumbered, the men got down on their knees and surrendered their weapons.

Ace, Darren, and Zane then went through each room off the main area looking for Kai. Ace wanted to break down right there when he realized that Kai was not there. He stood off to the side watching as Elijah and Darren restrained the three men. He didn't care what they did to the men, he needed to get back out there and find his daughter. He left out the building back to the car hearing the crew beating the men and looking for answers.

******

Dame sat in the backseat of the all black Suburban down the street from the old factory where the meeting was supposed to be held. There was about ten minutes before the scheduled meet time and he hadn't seen anyone arrive. He had hoped that Elijah would show up with everything he had asked for. His men were surrounding the whole building and he had instructed them to kill everyone on sight. He planned on taking the money and the recipe to Blue Wave, then taking over the city of Atlanta once again.

Twenty minutes passed and Dame hadn't seen any movement going towards the building. No one had walked or driven by at all. He hoped that Jesse had really placed the call to Elijah. He shook his head at how much of a fuck up his only son was. He felt no remorse or sadness about killing Jesse. He hoped that Jesse's mother would just bury him quietly and move on. Dame had nothing nice to say about

Jesse and would hate to have to fake emotion at the loss of his son.

Over the years he had tried so hard to show Jesse the rules of the game, but Jesse was soft and couldn't handle the simplest of tasks. He had too many emotions and always let them get in the way of his decisions. Dame had grown tired of trying to guide him the right way. He had begun grooming his daughter Nyah to take over for him one day. She was proving to be very capable at the job.

Dame picked up his phone to call one of his men to see what was going on. He was growing impatient and couldn't risk anything going wrong with the deal. He could almost smell the money coming in, if everything went according to his plan. He had no idea that at this very moment, the guys had already swept through the place and figured out his intentions. The phone rung one time before the call ended.

BOOM!

The truck rocked backward from the impact of the explosion. Dame dropped his phone as he watched the entire building go up in flames. He leaned forward to see if anyone had escaped. The building was too covered in flames and smoke to make out any signs of movement. He didn't see anyone running from the building, so he knew that there was no one left. He tapped his driver on the shoulder to let him know to pull off.

Dame rode in disbelief that he had lost 7 of his best men in that building. He had two people circling the building the whole night, just in case the crew tried anything. They hadn't reported any suspicious activity. He wasn't sure what exactly had gone wrong and unless someone had managed to escape, he would never know the truth. He called up his right hand, Sean, to let him know what just happened. He also let Sean know to move Kai and everyone else to the safe house. After hanging up with Sean, he placed another call.

"Everything good?" The caller answered.

"No. Something went wrong. We're headed to the safe house. Go on to plan B."

"Okay. I got you."

Chapter 3

"Get up. Follow me." A deep voice said.

Kai looked to the door and saw a tall man enter the room. He had skin the color of smooth dark chocolate with black eyes and long black dreads. He had muscles with large veins bulging out. Kai was hesitant to follow. No one had spoken to her in hours and she was starving. She felt like this was the part in scary movies where the victim died. She needed to stall long enough for Darren or someone to come for her. They had to have realized that she was missing by now.

"I said come on!"

"Where are we going?" Kai asked hesitantly.

He gave her a look that said do as I say. Kai stood and followed him. He led her up the stairs and out of the front door where a black town car was waiting. The driver stood impatiently holding the door open for Kai to get in. She was looking across the driveway at the trees and wondering if she should make a run for it. Had she not been five months pregnant, she definitely would have tried. Instead, she got in the car and buckled up her seatbelt.

Inside of the car was very nice. There was bottled water and plenty of snacks. There were heavy black curtains blocking the view to the driver as well as all the windows. Kai hadn't eaten at all in the last 8 hours, her stomach let out a loud growl. The man heard it and looked down at her. For the first time, he noticed her small baby bump. He had a conscience and the thought of starving a pregnant woman and holding her hostage was very sick to him. He instructed the driver to stop through Zaxby's before heading to the safe house.

"Thank you." Kai said softly. The thought of a chicken finger sandwich and fried mushrooms dripping in Zax sauce had her and the baby doing a happy dance. She decided to cooperate with whatever the guy wanted, he was clearly not going to harm her today. Maybe she could use him to get some information on why and where she was going to be held.

"Kai, by the way."

"You are aware that you have been kidnapped?" The guy snapped back. He knew if Dame wanted this girl dead, he was most likely the one that was going to pull the trigger. The less he knew about Kai and vice versa, the better.

******

An hour later, Dame pulled up to the safe house. He walked in the living to see the remainder of his men standing there. Sean shook his head letting Dame know there were no survivors from the explosion. Dame ignored everyone else in the room and walked to the bar to pour himself a shot of Jack. Everyone in the room was afraid to move. If Dame could kill his own son and not show any remorse, they knew that none of them were safe from his wrath. They chose to steer clear of him when he was upset or angry.

"Is the girl here?" Dame asked Sean, who just nodded. Sean was probably the only one in the room not scared of Dame. He had been around Dame long enough to know that he wouldn't do anything. What happened with Jesse was very rare. Dame always sent someone else to do his dirty work. It wouldn't have looked good if Dame had sent someone else to murder his son.

Dame poured himself another shot as he tried to gather his thoughts. Since Jesse and his men had screwed up and got the wrong girl, Kai was pretty much useless to them. He wanted things to end quickly so he could get back on top. Going to war with Elijah and his old connect would not be a good idea. He didn't have the resources or manpower for it.

He knew his other accomplice would be on their way to start plan B, but that would take some time to complete. He needed someone there beside him; someone just as ruthless as him and knew just as much about his enemy. He left the room and everyone standing there and went into his office. He placed a call to someone he hadn't spoken to in about 5 years.

"Hello?" She answered on the third ring.

"Livi baby, don't hang up." He said hopefully. The last few times he had tried to contact her, she had blew him off claiming she was through with her past. The clowns she kept marrying didn't know what to do with a woman like Olivia

Jackson-Malone, though. Dame was so in love with her and certain that he was the best man for her, but she didn't see it that way.

"What do you want, Dame?" She snapped.

"I got a new plan. I hear your *husband* is back in town." Dame was lying, but he figured Ace would have to show face sooner or later. There was no way his old partner would stay gone knowing his daughter was missing, or at least that's what Dame was counting on.

"I'm on my way." Olivia said then hung up.

Dame shook his head at her. Some might call him heartless, but he had nothing on Olivia. Any woman that would neglect her kids to chase behind a man or money should be ashamed of herself.

Chapter 4

Justice was growing tired of Elijah ignoring her. She had called him 15 times in a row and he had not bothered to answer or return any of her calls. Something could have been wrong with EJ or the new baby and he wouldn't know what was going on. She had tried everything she could think of to break him and this new girl up, but so far, nothing had worked. Elijah was still not trying to come back home to his family.

Once again she got up and ran racing to the restroom to throw everything up. Though she was well into her pregnancy, she was still getting sick and hated every minute of it. She had all these random cravings and when she couldn't get what she had been craving, her body rejected everything else. She was beyond tired all the time and chasing after a 2 year old was not making this pregnancy any easier for her. EJ was at the stage where if you left him alone for a minute, he was getting into something.

Yesterday, he had managed to untwist the cap off his sippy cup and poured it all over Justice's MacBook Air keyboard. She had spanked him on the butt one time and he screamed for his daddy for two hours straight. Justice had tried to call Elijah, but as usual, he didn't answer. Nothing she was doing to comfort him had worked. EJ cried for another thirty minutes before finally tiring himself out and falling asleep.

Tired of sitting around waiting, she got up and put some clothes on EJ. She was going to just show up on Elijah's doorstep. There would be no way he could ignore her then. After getting EJ and herself dressed, she grabbed her keys and walked out of the door to her 2014 Mercedes CLA250. Elijah had just purchased it for her. It was a cute car, but nothing like the $200,000 Bentley he had purchased for Khloé.

Arriving at Elijah's house 15 minutes later, Justice noticed him leaving to go somewhere. She stopped a couple of houses down and waited for him to get into his car. She watched as he locked the front door and walked to his car. He pulled out of his driveway and drove down the block before she made a U-turn and followed him.

He stopped at a liquor store before turning into a nice looking neighborhood in Virginia Highlands. He pulled into the driveway of a nice, modest, two-story home with a wraparound porch. She pulled in front of the neighbor's house and parked. It was close enough where she could see the front door without raising suspicion. She watched as a woman stepped onto the porch and greeted him wearing only a robe.

Tears involuntarily fell from Justice's eyes as she watched Elijah hug the woman then pick her up and carry her back inside. From the outside looking in, they looked like a loving couple. It made Justice sick to her stomach. She looked into the backseat and made sure EJ was still secured in his car seat before getting out. He was sleeping peacefully, oblivious to the fact that his father was ripping out his mother's heart. She locked the doors, but left the car running and walked up to the woman's door.

"ELIJAH!" Justice screamed banging on the wooden door. How could he do this to her? First with that bitch Khloé and now this hoe. She stepped back as the porch light came on and the door opened.

"Justice? What the fuck you doing here?" Elijah asked stepping outside fixing his belt and closing the door behind him.

"Exactly. What the fuck? First you leave your family for that Khloé bitch and now you out here chasing random hoes. I been at home sick as a fucking dog carrying your got damn child, calling you to come pick up your son, but you don't have time for that, right? You got time to be fucking, though! I see what the fuck this is!"

"You done? You already knew what this was. Go home man, I'll come get EJ later."

As Elijah turned to go back in the house, Justice grabbed his arm and tried to pull him back outside. Here she was standing in his face, and he was just going to ignore her and go back to fucking this little hoe again.

"Man, Justice, go on with the bullshit. You know we not rocking like that."

"I love you, can't you see that? Don't do this to me." She cried. Tears and mascara running down her caramel colored cheeks. She hated herself for how weak she was for him. She couldn't stop the tears if she wanted to. The pregnancy hormones had her all in her feelings.

Just as Elijah was going to respond, the front door opened and his new chick walked out.

"I'm going to have to ask both of you to leave. I told you, Eli, I don't do drama." She said calmly, folding her arms across her chest. Elijah noticed that she had put some clothes on.

"Nah, Justice was just leaving." He said pulling her back in the house with him leaving Justice on the front porch feeling stupid once again.

Justice couldn't believe he just did that to her. She went back to her car and popped the trunk. Taking out her aluminum baseball bat, she walked back to the house. She then went to work smashing out all of Elijah's car windows causing the alarm to sound. She smashed one of his hoe's windows and dented her car before running back to her car. She laughed as she pulled off. She could see Elijah and his chick running outside to see what all the noise was about. Justice honked the horn twice and waved as she passed by.

******

"What the fu—" Justice woke up startled as she felt cold water and ice being poured over her. She was about to reach for her knife that was tucked under her pillow when she recognized the figure standing over her. The words suddenly got caught in her throat. She could see the anger burning in his eyes. His jaw was clenched tightly. He was beyond pissed off at her actions.

"What would make you pull some dumb shit like that? That girl ain't have shit to do with you and for the last fucking time, I ain't ya man! I ain't never going to be! Get that shit through your head!" Elijah spat at her before walking out of her room.

Justice cried again at his words. Elijah had never spoken to her that way. She sat shivering from her cold, wet, clothes. The AC was blasting and making her even colder. She walked into her master bathroom to shower and change clothes. She stood in the shower allowing her tears to mix in with the water. She didn't want to believe it, but she felt like she had lost Elijah for good. Even though it was clear he was done, she just wasn't ready to let him go.

After changing into new pajamas and pulling her wet hair on top of her head, she went down the hall to check on EJ. She needed to wake him, feed him, and give him a bath. She panicked when she walked in his room and found his bed empty. She ran through the entire upstairs before racing to the stairs. The baby gate was open the front door was unlocked.

She ran to her room to grab her cell phone to call the police and Elijah.

"What you want, Justice?" Elijah snapped into the phone.

"EJ is gone!" She fell on her bed crying hysterically.

"I got my son so stop all that crying shit. You wanted a break. I'll bring him back when I'm good and ready. Don't bother calling me." He said then hung up.

Justice couldn't believe Elijah would do something so heartless. Throughout their history together, he had treated her with nothing but respect. Even after her hiding EJ from him, they had found a way to be cordial before Justice started pressuring him to be a family. She had been scared to death that something had happened to her baby. No mother should ever have to feel such pain. She gathered herself and climbed into bed, tears soaked her pillow as she cried herself to sleep.

Chapter 5

It had been a couple of weeks since they had any new leads on Kai's whereabouts. Ace and Darren refused to give up any hope that she was out there. They had combed the streets of Atlanta and several of the metro areas looking for her. It was hard for Darren to go out and search for her like he wanted because he still had Destiny and DJ to think about, but Ace searched around the clock. They were looking for any information on Dame, Jesse, or Kai's whereabouts. The reward Darren had offered up wasn't bringing in any useful information. Sad to say, but day by day the others were starting to lose hope on ever finding her.

Ace was slowly unraveling from the inside out. He hadn't eaten or slept that much in the last few weeks. His facial hair had grown out and he needed a haircut and line up badly. He had only stopped by Khloé's every now and then to shower and get in a nap. He didn't want her feeling abandoned by him popping in and out of her life again. The two had talked about his absence and agreed to work on their relationship once Kai was rescued and back home. He knew Khloé was the easier going one of the two and knew he had his work cut out for him once Kai was home. She wouldn't be as forgiving as her twin.

Ace was on his way to meet Dutch at his hotel. Dutch said they needed to talk and Ace was curious to find out why. He gave his rental to the valet and walked into the lobby of the grand hotel. The Georgian Terrace was one of the best and most expensive hotels in Atlanta. Its grand suites rivaled those at the Ritz Carlton and went for hundreds to thousands of dollars a night. Ace had his own money and knew the money Dutch was spending was like pocket change to the average person. Dutch's pockets ran deep. He walked towards the dining room and saw Dutch seated at the bar so he went to join him.

"What's good?" Ace said patting Dutch on the back and taking the seat next to him.

Dutch swallowed his shot of Jack and let the bartender know he wanted another. "Yo, I fucked up real bad a long time ago, and I don't know if they'll ever forgive me."

"How long you been drinking, man? And I don't know what you talking about. You not making any sense." Ace pushed his seat back. The smell of alcohol was seeping through Dutch's pores.

"I'm talking about Darren." Dutch downed another shot. "And maybe Zane. Them little niggas could be mine. You know I been around Darren forever, and I lost track of Zane years ago. They have no idea, man."

Ace was silent. He didn't know what to say. The whole situation was really fucked up. How could Dutch go this long and not get the truth? It pained Ace every day of the twelve years that he was away from his girls. They had no idea why he was there one day and then gone the next minute. He and Olivia had decided to just tell them he was going away for work, but he knew that didn't mean that much to them. They were so young and he could only imagine the ideas they had running through their minds about why their father had disappeared for so long.

"You ain't got to say nothing. I know it's fucked up. I just wasn't ready to deal with the shit when I was young. I stayed close to Darren, though, he was always good."

Ace signaled the bartender. With everything Dutch was saying, he felt like he needed a shot too.

"I'm going back up to New York for a minute, see if I can track down his ho ass mama and see what's up. Bitch was on crack the last I heard, but I don't want to go to him with the story if it's not true."

"You think if she was on crack, she will remember who she was fucking damn near 30 years ago?"

"Probably not. But that bitch was down bad way back when. I hope she don't be on no bullshit now."

"Good luck with that. Stay up." Ace said getting up. He felt bad for his boy, but Dutch really brought all this on himself. He should have been trying to figure this out when he first came across Darren and Zane. Other than getting a DNA test from the boys, Ace didn't see how tracking down Darren's mother would be any help.

Dutch sat at the bar for a few more rounds before he set out for his private plane and airstrip.

******

“Ayo, I got the contact for that nigga Dame.” Zane said as soon as Ace picked up the phone.

“Aight, bet. I’m ready to end all this bullshit.”

After getting Dame’s phone number from Zane, Ace went into Kai’s bedroom to place the call. The first time he called, the phone rang and went to voicemail. He called back twice before Dame picked up.

“Who the fuck is blowing up my damn phone?” Dame answers angrily.

“It’s Ace, nigga. You already know what it is. Give me a time and place.” Ace wasn’t one to waste time on bullshit ass, meaningless conversation. Dame knew exactly why Ace was calling, so there was no need for pleasantries. They set up a meet time to talk and hung up. Ace had two hours to kill before he had to go meet up with Dame. He decided to lay down and try to get in a quick nap.

Ace woke up an hour later and hit up Darren. He wanted Darren sitting outside the spot, so he could follow Dame when he left. Darren asked if he should bring more people just in case, but Ace said he knew Dame wouldn’t try anything. Ace knew Dame very well. Dame was just for show. He surrounded himself with a bunch of yes men that he overpaid and took advantage of. Dame's whole persona was something out of an urban fiction novel, completely based off fantasy and hardly any reality.

After setting up the plan, he went out on the balcony to smoke a cigarette. He heard the glass door slide open, but he didn't turn around to face her. He was still having a hard time facing Khloé knowing her sister was still out there somewhere and he was the reason behind it.

"Hey Daddy. I'm heading out to the lab. Don't worry, Elijah will be there." She kissed his cheek and rushed back out of the door not letting Ace get a word in.

Ace shook his head at his daughter. He didn't believe for a second that Khloé was going to the lab, he just hoped she would be safe. Elijah had already informed him that the lab had been shut down until further notice. He agreed with that decision. He knew he should stay out of Khloé's business, he just prayed she knew what she was doing. On second thought, he texted Elijah to look out for her anyways. Putting out his cigarette, he opened the glass door and went inside to prepare to meet Dame.

******

Two hours later Ace pulled up to Petey's on Covington Highway to meet up with Dame. Petey's was one of the worst bars in the city. It was dark and dingy on the inside. People never ordered from the bar, but snuck in their own liquor instead. Something was always popping off at the spot and the owner had been threatened to get shut down several times. Still, it was the best place to meet up. It would be loud and busy, so no one could overhear the conversation being held between the two ex-friends.

Ace walked into the bar cautiously checking his surroundings for any suspicious activities. After finding a seat in a booth in the corner, so he could watch the front door and back hallway at the same time, he checked the scene again. He turned down a drink from the shot girl as he watched the door waiting for Dame.

Ten minutes later Dame walked in with three other men and sat across from Ace. Ace had to laugh, Dame was always such a pussy. He couldn't go anywhere alone, he always needed some kind of backup. His choice to surround himself with lots of people had caused his name to pop up in a lot of conversations at the bureau. The people Dame surrounded himself with were often times informants or wouldn't hesitate to throw Dame under the bus. The only thing keeping Dame out of jail was lack of evidence and witnesses. Ace felt like Dame had someone on the inside, but had never known for sure.

Both men sat and stared at each other for the moment, hatred evident in their expressions.

"So what you call me here for?" Dame was the first to speak up. He absentmindedly toyed with the gold Presidential

Rolex that gleamed around his wrist like he wasn't interested in anything Ace had to say.

"Don't play dumb. You know what the fuck this is and how I bring it. You got my daughter. I need to know what the fuck you want so I can bring her home." Ace pounded the table with his fist.

"I want to control Atlanta again. Your daughters' little boyfriends supposed to be running shit now. Ask them to step off and the little bitch can come home."

Ace punched Dame with a powerful right hook across his jaw causing it to crack. He then wrapped his large hands around Dame's throat choking him. Dame could say whatever, but Ace wasn't about to let him sit there and disrespect his daughter by calling her out of her name. The guys with Dame tried to pry Ace's fingers from Dame, but he had such a strong hold. Ace was determined to choke the life out of Dame with his bare hands. Ace heard a gun click behind his head as one of the guys placed a gun to the back of his head. He released Dame who immediately began gasping for air.

Ace looked around the bar and all eyes were on him. Seeing that the drama was over, people started slowly going back about their business playing pool or dancing. Something stayed popping off inside the bar so the customers were very used to it. Ace saw the bartender heading in their direction. The bartender was trying to get them out before the situation escalated any further. There had been two shootings at the bar in the last week and Rockdale County Police were already threatening to take his liquor license and shut him down for good.

"I'm going to have to ask y'all to leave." He stated calmly.

Ace was the first to gather himself and exit the restaurant. He knew he wouldn't get any more information from Dame. He knew Dame was only going home to plot on him some more. As he drove out of the parking lot, Ace texted Darren to make sure he was following Dame back to where he was keeping Kai. He was ready to bring his daughter home and take care of Dame for good this time.

When Ace got back to the twins' condo, he began to feel guilty for his actions. He had reacted foolishly and prayed it didn't cause Dame to bring any harm to Kai or his grandchild before he had a chance to make things right with her. He sat and smoked a blunt waiting on a call from Darren.

Chapter 6

After catching his breath, Dame gathered himself and exited the restaurant. The ride back to the safe house was silent as his two guards were scared to make a move. They knew how Dame's temper could be. They'd both messed up by allowing Ace to get his hands on Dame and they were sure they'd pay for it sooner or later. Dame sat in the back seat steaming mad. He vowed that was the last time Ace would get the best of him ever again.

Twenty minutes later, they pulled up in front of the safe house. The driver jumped as his partner slumped over and his head hit the dashboard. Dame shot him in the back of his head with a silencer on his gun before getting out of the car. The driver looked from the hole in the headrest of the seat to the blood splatter and brain matter now on the inside of the car's windshield. His knuckles turned white as he gripped the steering wheel trying not to retaliate.

"Torch this shit." Dame instructed before closing the door and walking away towards the house. He entered the front door and headed straight to his office, not bothering to acknowledge anyone along the way. Sitting at his desk he contemplated what his next move should be. His only connection to the drug, Blue Wave, was through Jesse to Khloé. Now that Jesse was dead, he had no other way of luring Khloé to him. He also knew that since Ace was back in town, there would be no way of just grabbing her. Going after the two boyfriends would be a dead end as well. According to his source, neither one showed their face on the streets that often. He was just about to call in Sean to take Kai home when he heard the sounds of heels clicking towards the door.

His office door swung opened and there stood the devil herself, Olivia Jackson-Malone. She was the most gorgeous white woman he'd ever come across. She stood 5'6 with long platinum blonde dyed hair that she wore bone straight with a part down the middle. Her blue eyes were cold as ice and would darken when she was angry. She hardly smiled and always wore a serious expression on her face. She had fake 36C breasts and Dame noticed she had also gotten some ass shots, making her hips and ass look more round.

"What's up, Livi?" Dame stood and walked to her, grabbing her into a hug.

"No one calls me Livi anymore." She said hugging him back.

He sat back behind his desk and she took a seat on the edge. A flood of emotions ran through him as he continued to take her in. She was wearing a tight knee length black pencil skirt, a black shirt, and blazer. Always having the most expensive tastes, Louboutin's graced her feet and she placed her Birkin bag on his desk. It had been about 5 years since he last laid eyes on her and she was more beautiful than he remembered. He reminisced on how she had always snuck out on him after they made love.

Dame had fallen asleep after the last round of coke and sex he just shared with Olivia. She was the true definition of a freak. He'd never experienced sex as good as hers. He hoped that since Ace hadn't returned since he left a year ago, he could sweep in and make her his woman. Olivia hadn't expressed any deeper feelings towards him, but he knew her money supply was probably running dry without Ace. A woman like Olivia did not work and expected to be kept. He wouldn't say that he loved her, but he felt like taking Ace's woman would be a huge boost to his own ego.

Dame felt the bed shift and laid there pretending to sleep as he hoped she was ready for another round. Instead he heard the bathroom door open and the light come on. Olivia was using the light from the bathroom to gather up her belongings. She had slept with Dame because he always talked too much. She was hoping to get information about Ace's whereabouts.

Just yesterday, she had received divorce papers in the mail from Ace. Dame had called her and she met him at their usual spot. He always brought the coke and though he wasn't much to look at, he had a mean dick game. After doing a bunch of lines and going for three rounds and not getting any info, Olivia was ready to go home. Ace had been sending checks in the mail for the twins and paying all the bills, but he hadn't shown his face in about a year. Olivia couldn't wait to see him again, he would regret the day he ever abandoned her.

Dame watched as she put on her shirt inside out and snuck out of the hotel room door. He laid back on the bed. He wasn't worried at all by her sudden exit. She'd be his one day, he was sure of it. He fell back asleep with replays of their sexual encounter running through his mind.

"So why is my ex-husband back in town this time?" Olivia asked bringing Dame out of his lustful thoughts.

"Well…" He wasn't really sure how to tell her that he had kidnapped her pregnant daughter. Olivia played the bad bitch role, but he knew her daughters were still her weakness. She pretended to hate them and be jealous, but she was a damn good mother to those girls, until recently. "There was a situation involving my son and your daughter. You know Jesse has always been a fuck up. He attempted to kidnap your Khloé and ended up getting her sister instead."

Olivia took in what he was saying. She knew he wasn't telling the whole story truthfully, but honestly she didn't care. She knew Ace loved those girls more than anything in the world. The only reason he'd stayed away so long, was because Olivia had threatened to go to the bureau and tell his bosses of the drug money he had stacked offshore. The thought of life in prison would scare anyone straight.

Dame had poisoned Olivia's mind about why Ace had left all those years ago. Initially, she understood why Ace had to go, but after the months turned to years, she felt he was being selfish. It was Dame who had told Olivia about the offshore money and how he had overthrown Dame by stealing his plug. Olivia couldn't believe Ace had abandoned their family for drugs. Was being a kingpin that important to him? The only contact she had with him was when it had something to do with the girls. Olivia had begun to resent her daughters for those very reasons.

The fact that Ace didn't feel like he had to share with her why he was abandoning their family so suddenly still bothered her to this day. She had to sleep with Dame twice before he gave up any good information. She didn't regret her decision for a minute after everything she'd learned. Her marriage was already fizzling out before Ace left. She just didn't understand why Ace never fought for their relationship more.

Ace had spent most of his time running the streets, playing drug dealer, and chasing behind loose women. Any spare time he had, he spent spoiling the girls and taking them places. When she found out the truth from Dame, it had hurt her to her core. She could be cold hearted most of the time, but the love she felt for Ace was real. She'd been out to his house in California once in the last 12 years, but she didn't have the heart to beg him to come home. When she returned back to Atlanta and he continued to stay away, she had a change of heart and began plotting against him. She was ready for him to feel how he had torn her heart to a million pieces all those years ago.

"You have my daughter where?" Olivia asked with a feigned attitude.

"She's safe, don't worry. We have her very comfortable. No harm has come to her at all. She and the baby are doing fine." Dame tried to reassure her. He saw her ice blue eyes darken with anger.

"Baby? You mean to tell me your son kidnapped my daughter and she is pregnant with my grandchild!" Olivia kept pretending to be upset. If Ace knew that Kai was pregnant, he was probably going crazy looking for her. Ace being off his game was just what Olivia and Dame needed to carry out their plans. Ace would come to them, and they'd be ready to ambush him. Dame had his reasons for wanting Ace gone and Olivia had hers.

"Yes… but like I said, she's perfectly safe." Dame tried to explain.

"Take me to her right now!" Olivia commanded. She needed to make sure Kai was really being taken care of. She didn't want any harm brought to her or her grandchild.

Dame hesitated for a moment. He wasn't sure that was a good idea. He didn't know what Olivia's plans were. He couldn't allow her to free Kai until he came up with a new plan. Olivia always acted impulsively and reacted without thinking the situation through. In order to bring Ace down, he need her to slow down and plan things out carefully.

Olivia sensed the hesitation in Dame. She stood from his desk and opened the door to his office. She began walking through the halls shouting Kai's name. Dame was right on her heels trying to get her to calm down and think rationally.

"Livi, wait. Think of how this can help us. Ace will come to us. We just have to be patient."

His pleas fell on deaf ears as Olivia continued on her way.

******

Kai was growing tired of being locked in the room all day. After she was moved to the new location, the tall, handsome man, whose name she later found out was Sean, had put her in a comfortable little room and left her there. She had a decent queen sized bed, a huge TV mounted on the wall, and a small fridge with snacks. Someone brought her dinner every evening, and she was even allowed to have some of her pregnancy cravings. Even though she was being treated nicely, she was more than ready to return home and be with Darren and the twins. She also missed her twin so much, they had never been apart for this long in 21 years.

Just as Kai was about to go knock on the door to ask if she could maybe go for a walk, she heard shouting. She placed her ear to the door to hear what was going on. Maybe Darren had come for her? She stepped back and ran her fingers through her red hair. She looked down at the velour Walmart sweat suit one of the guards had brought her to change into a couple of days ago. She hoped she looked okay. She knew it was silly to be worried about such trivial things, but she hadn't seen her man in a couple of weeks.

The last time she saw him, they were fighting. She couldn't wait to apologize and make up with him. Shouting brought her out of her vain thoughts. She couldn't make out what was happening on the other side of door, but she could hear a familiar woman's voice and a man getting closer.

"Open this door right now!"

Kai thought her mind was playing tricks on her. She hadn't been gone that long, but it sounded like her mother's voice.

Kai backed away from the door slowly and sat on the bed. The wind had literally been knocked out of her as she came face to face with her mother for the first time in three years.

Olivia looked from the shocked and hurt look on Kai's face to her small, round, protruding baby bump. She couldn't believe Kai was that far along and hadn't even called to mention the pregnancy or her relationship with the baby's father. Olivia should have felt guilty for missing out on her daughters' lives and them not feeling comfortable enough to call her, but all she felt was anger and jealousy. The twins could reach out to her just as much as she could call them. They rarely called unless it was something they needed her to co-sign on or pay for.

Before either Kai or Olivia could speak, gunshots could be heard coming from outside the house. Dame, Olivia, and Kai stared at each other for a brief moment before they all rushed down the hall and out the front door to see what was going on. When they all reached the front porch, they stopped dead in their tracks. Sean was dragging a body to the driveway where a car was parked. He didn't acknowledge them as he walked around the car and popped the trunk.

"What the fuck happened here?" Dame was the first to speak. The last thing they needed was to be drawing attention to themselves way out in country ass Conyers. These country white people wouldn't hesitate to hang them for a murder.

"Saw him creeping along the side of the house. When I approached him, he pulled his gun. I shot first though." Sean said nonchalantly while pulling out a clear tarp from the trunk to wrap the body in.

Kai walked awkwardly behind her mother and Dame as they approached the car. She noticed how unbothered her mother seemed by the dead body on the ground before them. Kai looked across the driveway to the neighbor's house and wondered if she could make it there before anyone noticed she was missing. The baby started moving in her stomach making her ditch that idea and look down. On the way down, her eyes locked on the face of the body.

"NOOOOOOOO!" She screamed hysterically before vomiting everything she'd eaten today onto the driveway.

Olivia, Sean, and Dame all looked at her with confused expressions. She kneeled by the body and hugged him close. Her heart was broken and her words were muffled by her cries. No one could make out what she was saying. Sean attempted to pull her off of the body, but she wouldn't let go. She was drawing unnecessary attention to herself and would alert the neighbors.

"No! Don't touch me! Don't touch him!" She cried. "Why? WHY HIM?"

Dame went back into the house. Kai's screams were annoying him. The guy was dead. There was nothing else they could do about it. He was slightly upset it wasn't Ace laying there on his driveway. He hadn't checked to see if he followed him from the bar. Things could have gone worse if Ace had managed to track them down.

Olivia watched on as Kai cried for the man. She could see the pain in Kai's eyes. Her eyes had turned to a light gray color. She could tell by the way Kai was screaming, that she loved him. Olivia knelt down and checked for a pulse on the body's wrist before standing up and whispering instructions to Sean.

"Kai, baby, you have to let him go. We need to get him to the hospital." Olivia said gently, trying to get Kai to let the man go.

"No, he's gone. You killed him! He's gone. Why did you do this?" She was so distraught.

"He's got a pulse. It's just really faint." Olivia coaxed. "If you don't let him go, they can't save him. He's losing blood quickly."

At those words, Kai reluctantly let him go. Sean picked him up and put him in the back seat of the car before closing the door. Kai tried to open the passenger side door, but it was locked. She looked from her mother to Sean in confusion.

"I need to go with him! Open the door!" She pleaded. Sean ignored her cries as he climbed in the driver seat and started the car. Olivia pulled Kai back and held her as she broke down. Sean pulled off.

"I need to go! Please, I need to know if he's okay." She cried to her mother.

"I'm sure he'll be fine." Olivia said before turning to walk inside. "Come inside."

Kai looked longingly back at the neighbor's house. If she wasn't nervous that she'd fall and hurt her baby, she'd take her chances in running. She looked back at the house and saw a guard watching her. He probably would catch her before she made it halfway across the yard. Defeated, she held her head down and walked back into the house. This time, she locked herself in her bedroom. She sunk to the floor and broke down crying. Through her tears, she said a prayer for her baby's father. She prayed that God would spare his life and bring him back to her. Her heart said everything would be fine, but her mind said otherwise.

Chapter 7

Khloé was laughing uncontrollably as she shot basketball after basketball. This was the most fun she'd had since Kai went missing. Initially, she had felt guilty for going out and having fun while her sister could be out there somewhere, possibly getting tortured, but now she had to admit she was actually enjoying herself. She had been sitting in her lab wondering what to do next when she got a call from Malik. He had talked her into coming out so that he could cheer her up. They had been going back to back in games of Basketball Shootout at Dave and Buster's. She had won three times in a row and he kept trying to win. For someone so athletic, he had no aim. She hadn't laughed this much in weeks.

After beating him a fourth time, they decided to call it quits and grab something to eat. Malik watched Khloé's hips and ass sway in her light blue, distressed H&M jeans as she walked towards the food area. He liked that she was simple and could put on some jeans and sneakers and have a good time. He hoped whatever she had going on with ole boy from their first date was over. They sat at a booth near the bar and waited for the waiter to come along.

Khloé picked up her phone to check her messages, but all she saw was 5 missed calls from Elijah. She rolled her eyes, she was hoping for a text letting her know they'd found Kai.

Elijah had been blowing her up all day, but she had no reason to speak to him. He needed to be more concerned about his little family with Justice and EJ and leave her alone. She still wasn't feeling a romantic connection with Malik, but he was a cool friend to have around.

"Everything good?" Malik asked noticing the change in her body language.

"Yeah. Just waiting on my father to call." Khloé said brushing off the subject of Elijah. "How's everything going with your gym?"

"It's going good. I'm too geeked about finally getting my own space. It's been a dream of mine. I hated paying to use other people's spaces for my clients." Malik had just received a grant and a microloan from the Small Business Association to open up his very own gym. He had just found a nice space on a good part of town that only needed minor remodeling. He was hoping to open by the end of the year, which was just about 5 months away. With his own space, he could take on more clients and even bring in some of his other trainer friends.

Khloé admired the fact that Malik was into such a legit business. At first she found him boring, and the way he backed down to Elijah that time had turned her completely off of him, but over time she started to see him as a cool person. He was very smart and funny. It also didn't hurt that he was extremely handsome.

His green eyes did something to her. She felt like she could talk to him about anything. He seemed to cater to whatever she needed without her having to say a word. This was only their first date since Kai went missing, but she could see him making some girl very happy one day. They texted and spoke on the phone almost every day. He was even encouraging her to get back in the lab. She had tried, but was nervous that her ideas would only cause more pain than good.

It had never been her intention to make drugs. The money that Blue Wave made her was too enticing. She had grown up spoiled and had everything she needed, but there was nothing like having your own money. She watched Kai work and always admired that her sister was making her own money. Khloé would never have the confidence to go out and model, but the lab was her home. Making Blue Wave had her feeling like she could really do something amazing with her life. But all it had done was turn her best friend against her and get her sister kidnapped.

"You always zone out on me. What's on your mind, shawty?" Malik asked sitting back into the booth. He had been talking to her for a minute, but it didn't seem like she was listening. He could tell something had been on her mind all day and he wanted her to feel like she could open up to him. He felt like Khloé could be the girl for him, she was everything any man could want and more, but it didn't seem like she could see it.

"Just got a lot going on. My dad came back in town after being gone a long time. I haven't talked to my sister in a while." Khloé said not really wanting to go into the details about Kai's disappearance.

Malik didn't say anything. He could tell she didn't really want to talk about it. He wasn't really good at giving advice and always felt as though things would work themselves out. He didn't know the full story and unless she wanted him to know, he wouldn't pry. He watched as her facial expression changed as her phone lit up again. He hoped it wasn't her ex, but whoever it was had been blowing her up all day. He knew he couldn't be the only man vying for Khloé's attention, but he couldn't help feeling the jealousy.

"You want to handle that?" He suggested.

"Yeah. Sorry, it will be quick." Khloé grabbed her phone, walked out of the building, and picked up the call. "What Elijah?"

"You need to get up to Grady ASAP. Darren got shot." Elijah sounded upset.

"I'm on my way." Khloé turned around to go back in to tell Malik she was leaving, but he was right behind her. He had picked her up, so she didn't have her car.

"Can you drop me off at Grady? Something happened to my sister's boyfriend." Khloé asked already walking to Malik's car.

Malik followed behind her hitting the unlock button on his car. They climbed in and he pulled off towards the hospital.

The ride was silent and he could tell Khloé seemed anxious about something. He grabbed her hand and held it in attempt to calm her down. She gave him a half smile to say she was grateful for him being there. When they pulled up to emergency, she hopped out of the car without saying a word to him. She was more concerned about what happened with Darren. If something had happened to him before Kai came home, Kai would be devastated.

"What happened?" Khloé asked Elijah when she walked into the waiting. He was the first person she noticed as he was up pacing the floor.

"We don't know. The twins' grandmother is a nurse here, and she said someone dropped him off outside the doors and sped off. He got shot twice." Elijah said solemnly. Darren was his only family, he couldn't take it if something happened to him.

Khloé wrapped her arms around him and hugged him tightly. She knew he needed to be comforted. Though she had decided she couldn't be with him right now, she still cared for him deeply. They hadn't called it love, but she could see herself loving him. She felt his body tense and a throat clear behind her. She turned to see who it was and came face to face with Malik. She hadn't expected him to come inside.

"What the fuck you doing here?" He recognized Malik as the guy Khloé went on a date with a while back. "This a family issue. You not welcome here."

Malik took notice as Elijah pulled Khloé behind him as if he were staking his claim. He also took note that Khloé didn't make a move to come around him. She had already chosen without speaking a word.

"I was just bringing Khloé her phone, she left it in my car when I dropped her off." Malik didn't come here to fight anybody. He had sent her a text to call him if she needed anything and her phone beeped in the car.

"Thanks. Bye, little nigga." Elijah snatched the phone from Malik's hand then turned and faced Khloé who had an angry look on her face. Elijah was mad at the fact that Khloé was even out with this clown. She couldn't pick up the phone when he called because she was out smiling with the next nigga. Khloé definitely had him fucked up.

"Why you acting like that? He didn't do nothing to you." Khloé said before walking away to go catch up to Malik.

"You really going to chase after that nigga?" Elijah grabbed her arm and pulled her back. The fact that she was just going to leave him when he needed her there. His only family might not make it and the only thing she could think to do is go explain herself to the next nigga.

Khloé could see the hurt mixed with anger in his deep brown eyes. A part of her wanted to comfort him, but he was wrong this time. He had no right to speak to Malik that way. They were not together. She could speak to and go out with whomever she wanted. She turned and walked away catching up to Malik. Elijah would just have to get over it.

"Sorry about that. He doesn't get that whatever we had is over." Khloé explained once she caught up to Malik. She didn't want him to feel like Elijah was an issue in their friendship.

"No worries. We good, shawty. Hit me up when you get some time." He kissed her on the forehead then walked away.

Khloé stood and watched him walk away. She felt like she should say something more, but she didn't know what to say exactly. For some reason she felt like this moment was more like a good bye than a see you later. Every date she had been on with Malik had somehow been wrecked by Elijah. Angry, she turned and walked back to the waiting room.

"You have no right to keep doing that! I am not your girl. What we had is over. Go be with your baby mama or whoever else you probably sleeping around with and leave me the fuck alone!" She then went and sat in a chair next to her father. Her honey colored skin flushed red with anger. She laid her head on his shoulder as they waited for the doctor to come out.

Before Elijah could go speak with Khloé and apologize, Jazzy showed up with the twins. Elijah had tried to get in contact with Camryn to come get the kids, but she hadn't answered her cell phone. He had asked Ms. Pam if she had been in contact with Cam, but had been told Camryn hadn't seen the kids in months and couldn't care less about them or Darren. The twins had been staying with her after school until Darren got off of work at the studio.

"Family of Darren Price." A short Indian doctor called out.

Elijah and Khloé walked up to him while the kids and Jazzy joined Zane and Ace in the waiting room. Khloé took notice how Jazzy had found a seat in Zane's lap instead of the empty chair next to him.

"What's the word doc?" Elijah was the first to speak.

"He had two shots to his upper body. One in the chest missed his heart by an inch and went through his back narrowly missing his spine. The other went through his stomach missing all his vital organs. We were able to repair all the damages, but he lost a lot of blood. We gave him a transfusion. He's resting now, you may go see him two at a time. Be advised, he needs his rest." The doctor informed them then walked away.

They both exhaled at the news. Khloé turned to go back and sit with her father, but Elijah pulled her back. He couldn't go see his brother like that alone. He needed his girl by his side. Though he and Khloé were not together anymore, he felt like it was only a matter of time before they worked things out. He had already claimed her as his future wife. He just needed her to fall in line.

The two walked hand in hand down the hall to Darren's room. They watched from the door as he slept peacefully. Khloé was kind of glad that Kai wasn't there. She knew her twin would be flipping out so much right now. Darren was all bandaged up.

Elijah couldn't handle seeing his brother like that. He couldn't wait for Darren to wake up so he could find out what happened and who did this to him. He took a seat next to Darren's bed. Khloé squeezed Elijah's shoulder before giving them some privacy. She walked back to the waiting room to tell everyone how Darren was doing.

Chapter 8

Darren's eyes flickered open for a moment. He shut them quickly, the lights in the room were too bright. He looked around the room and noticed he was in a hospital room. He immediately began to panic. The last thing he remembered was being shot by someone when he was trying to save Kai. He had looked through the window and down a hallway. He saw her standing between two figures, her stomach had grown out a little since he last saw her.

Kai… He suddenly began to panic. He pulled the heart rate monitor from his finger causing a machine to beep loudly. He tore the IV out of his arm and attempted to sit up, but fell back due to a shooting pain in his chest. He braced himself and attempted to sit back up, but failed again. He couldn't sit here, he had to get to his girl.

"Calm down, yo. Where the fuck you trying to go?" Elijah came into the room and pushed Darren back down on the bed. A nurse was right behind him to reattach the heart rate monitor on his finger. The machine stopped beeping as it registered his pulse. She then went to work setting up to reinsert his IV as well.

"Kai…" Darren attempted to explain, but fell into a coughing fit from tightness in his chest. The nurse went to the sink and got him a cup of water. He drank it down in one gulp. Elijah took the cup and refilled it for him.

"She's still gone, bruh." Elijah said not wanting to go into detail in front of the nurse. He knew how much Darren cared for Kai. He hated to have to be the one to give him the bad news.

Neither one said anything else as they waited for the nurse to finish up and leave the room. She asked Darren a few questions about his pain level. Elijah sent a text to Ace and Zane to come up to the hospital. Just as Elijah was getting ready to kick the nurse out for moving so slow, two men in suits walked in flashing their badges.

"Darren Price? I'm Detective Hill and this is my partner Detective White, Atlanta PD. We have a couple questions for you." Detective Hill was a tall slim man. He was well over six feet with brown skin and a shiny bald head. He had a pencil thin mustache and goatee. Detective White was a heavy set man who kind of resembled Carl Winslow from the show Family Matters.

"I don't know what happened. I got knocked out and then I woke up here." Darren said to the detectives.

"Do you remember where you were? And do you know anyone that would want to harm you?" Detective Hill asked not believing a word Darren had just said.

"No." Darren said not wanting to give them any information. He planned to get his own street justice later. He was already plotting on how he would kill the mother fucker who shot him. As soon as he got out of this hospital bed.

"Well, we know you just woke up. If you remember anything else, just give us a call." Detective Hill said attempting to hand Darren his card. When Darren didn't reach out to take it, he sat it on his food tray and walked out with his partner right behind him.

Elijah and Darren sat in silence for a minute making sure the detectives were gone before either of them spoke. The nurse had finally finished up and was on her way out as well.

"So where she at?" Ace asked walking in the room. He was glad Darren was awake and doing well, but it was way past time to bring Kai home.

"This house out in Conyers. Track my car, it is parked two houses down from the place." Darren tried to sit up once again, but the pain was too intense. Realizing he wasn't going to be able to go, he laid back down feeling defeated. "Bring her straight here."

"I got you, bruh. Sit your cripple ass down. We got this." Elijah stood and dapped Darren before leaving the room with Ace right behind him. He knew Darren wanted to be there, but he was no good to anybody hurt like that. He would just be in the way.

******

Dutch looked on as Darren slept. He had watched him grown from the time he was 12 years old until he was the man lying in bed before him. When Dutch had seen the path Darren was going down, robbing stores and people for food and money, he stepped in. At first he just wanted to provide him some guidance, but Darren couldn't keep himself out of trouble.

Dutch then started teaching him the drug game. Dutch was young and stupid and should have done way better by Darren, but living the fast life he was living, he didn't think of anyone but himself. He had only heard rumors of Darren being his son. Though there was strong resemblance, he didn't buy into it. He wanted to ignore it because he wasn't ready for a child. The more he was around Darren, the more he could see himself in him. Still, he had never brought up his suspicions to Darren or anyone else.

For the last two weeks Dutch had been to Brooklyn to try and track down Darren's mother, Peaches. Just when he got an address on her, he got the call Darren was shot. He immediately rushed and hopped on a plane to come see about him. He had paid for a paternity test while Darren was still under for the surgery. He spared no expense for having the results back quickly. He sat in the room holding the envelope the nurse gave him unsure of if he wanted to open it before he spoke with Darren or after.

"Why you looking like someone died?" Darren was up and looking at Dutch. He wondered where everyone else was. He had woken up a few times and was growing anxious. They should have been back with Kai by now.

"They went for Kai. Ms. Pam went to get your kids situated in bed. The guys will text when they on the way back." Dutch said as he read the results saying he was 99.6% the father of Darren Deshawn Price. He laughed at the fact that Peaches gave Darren his first name as his middle name. He was pleased to see they shared a last name, at least she did that right.

"You good old man? You seem like you losing it." Darren joked.

Dutch got up and handed him the paper. He watched as Darren's face went from question to anger as he read the results and threw them back at him.

"Get out. Don't say shit." Darren said calmly. This was some bullshit. "Leave."

"You don't have any questions? I didn't know for sure. I—" Dutch started to explain.

"GO NIGGA!" Darren said trying to get up to kick Dutch out himself. The machines started going off as his blood pressure became elevated. He couldn't believe the bullshit Dutch was telling him. He'd known Dutch for 13 years and never once had Dutch said anything about possibly being his father. Back when Camryn had just given birth, Darren had confided in Dutch that he never had a family and wasn't sure he'd be a good father to the twins. Dutch had assured him he would be an excellent father, knowing this whole time that he had never been much of a father to Darren. How could he give advice on being a father when he hadn't been a good one himself?

Sure Dutch had saved him and Elijah from the destructive path they were on. But Dutch had been in the neighborhood for years before putting them on. Darren had slept on the same pissy mattress for 5 years, getting all sorts of rashes and infections. His clothes were always dirty and worn out. He always badly needed a haircut. His thick, curly hair was always pulled back in a nappy ponytail. The kids at school teased him relentlessly. He stayed fighting older boys for bullying him. His mother never cared, she was always more concerned about chasing behind men and then eventually she got hooked on the drugs.

Nurses rushed in trying to get Darren to calm down, but he wouldn't. He wanted Dutch out of his room. Dutch was just standing there looking sorry. For the first time, Darren noticed the resemblance between the two. They had the same hazel eyes and nose. Their height and build was the same. He didn't know why he never noticed it before. Suddenly he felt a calm wash over him as the nurse pushed a sedative into his IV and everything went black.

Chapter 9

Elijah and Ace crept to the backdoor of the two story brick home. They had about six of Elijah's team with them. Two of the guys, Black and Mitch, were going around the front of the house. The plan was to kick in both doors at the same time, not allowing anyone to escape. Ace wanted a blood bath for Dame having the audacity to touch his daughter. Anyone associated with Dame had to pay the price with their life. They had watched the house for the last two hours, waiting for it to get dark outside.

Once the sky was dark and they were sure how many were inside, they kicked in the backdoor and went in guns first. Seconds after they entered, the front door came crashing down as well. They could see three of Dame's guards scrambling to get their weapons. Sean, Dame, and another man were all seated at the table eating when they burst in.

Elijah pointed two guns at Sean. He looked like the man Darren had described as his shooter. Black put a gun to the back of Dame's head as the rest of Elijah's team disarmed and lined up Dame's men. Ace's focus was solely on finding Kai. He went down the hall and up the staircase calling Kai's name.

"Kai… Kai, baby girl." He called out.

Kai was sitting up on the edge of the bed trying to figure out a place to hide. She had heard the commotion downstairs and didn't know what to expect. She thought she heard someone calling out her name, but she was sure she was imagining things. She wiped the snot from her nose. Her eyes were all puffy, red, and swollen from crying. She had been crying nonstop since Sean drove away with Darren's body. She had convinced herself that he was dead, and she was going to be stuck raising her baby alone, *if it turned out to be his.* She cried for the twins. They were so young and both their parents would no longer be in their lives.

"Kai." She heard the voice call out to her from outside the door.

"In here." She called out glumly. She didn't care to fight anymore. Without Darren, she didn't really care if she lived or not.

"Stand back baby girl." Ace shouted out to her as he stood back and prepared to kick the door in.

Kai hadn't even bothered to move from where she sat. She watched as the door flew off the hinges. She broke down crying again at the sight of her father. It had been almost a month since she was taken and she wasn't sure she was ever going to be out of there. She wasn't mistreated, she just missed her family. She cried harder because she realized she was returning home to nothing, her man wouldn't be there.

"Hey baby. We gotta go, you good?" Ace spoke softly, looking over her for any cuts or bruises. His heart was breaking again at how broken she looked. He could tell she had been crying. She didn't look like she'd been physically harmed in any way. As he hugged her tightly, he vowed to do everything in his power from this moment forward to make sure that both of his daughters always stayed smiling. He picked her up like a child and carried her back down the hall and out of the front door to the waiting car.

"Is he dead?" Kai held onto her father's shirt. Before she left, she had to know the truth. She needed to prepare herself along the ride if she had to view his body or plan a funeral. She wasn't sure she could look his kids in the eyes and tell them their father wasn't coming back.

"No. He's waiting for you." Ace said then kissed her forehead and closed the door. Mitch pulled off to take Kai to the hospital as Ace went back inside.

Just as he crossed over the threshold he heard several shots and bodies drop. He saw two guys in the kitchen disconnecting the stove. Elijah instructed the other three to take Sean and Dame back to the warehouse and wait for him there. Ace watched how in control Elijah seemed of the whole situation. Though he was mad at Darren for allowing his daughter to get taken, he knew both Elijah and Darren were good guys. His daughters had chosen well.

Everybody filed out of the house and into the awaiting vehicles. Black was the last one to exit the house. The tires screeched as Elijah pulled off down the long driveway. There was a loud boom behind them causing the car to jerk forward a little bit from the explosion.

******

Kai couldn't speak, she just stood in the doorway of Darren's hospital room and watched him sleep. She didn't care that her ponytail was loose and the rubber band was falling off. She didn't care that her face was all puffy and red from crying. She couldn't believe that he was alive and laying there. He had come to save her, but she didn't know what that meant. Before everything went down, they had gotten into a bad fight. She knew now that she loved him and wanted a life with him, but she wasn't sure how he felt. He could have only come for her on the strength that her child could be his. Not sure if she could face possible rejection, she just stood and watched him.

Darren felt someone watching him as he slept. He opened his eyes and stared at her for a moment. Even dressed in a cheap sweat suit and hair all over her head, Kai was still beautiful. Her blue eyes looked like she had been crying and that made him feel like shit. Instead of fighting with her over some bullshit, he was supposed to be protecting her. When he found out that she had been taken, their fight seemed so small and stupid. He had already forgiven her for talking to her ex. They still needed to talk, but right now he just needed to hold her in his arms.

"Sorry." They both said at the same time then laughed awkwardly.

Kai climbed in the bed with him as tears fell from her eyes. She thanked God for sparing his life and allowing them to be back together. She felt silly for spending the last two days planning to be a single mother and dying alone. She laid her head on his chest and then jumped back as Darren winced in pain.

Darren pulled her back to him. Even though she was smashing him and causing him pain, he had waited weeks to hold her. Nothing else mattered at the moment. He kissed her on the forehead and closed his eyes. They both drifted off to sleep together.

Chapter 10

"So what's the move?" Darren asked climbing into the passenger side of Elijah's Escalade. It had been a week since they'd rescued Kai and about a day since he'd been home from the hospital. He was happy for Kai to be home, but it was time to get down to business. He knew that the guys were holding Dame and Sean for him at the warehouse. His mind was racing a mile a minute at the thought of killing the two men.

"You good?" Elijah could see the murder dancing in Darren's hazel eyes. He handed him a sack of weed and a cigar so he could roll a blunt to calm his nerves.

"Yeah." Darren said lighting the blunt.

Forty-five minutes later they were pulling up outside the warehouse. No words were spoken as they approached the building. Black and another dude were standing watch outside the door. They nodded at them to say what's up. They could hear the sounds of Dame and Sean being beat by the crew as they walked in the door.

Darren didn't speak. When he was about to put down his murder game, he preferred silence. He always thought out every step. The whole time she was missing, he realized how much he loved Kai. Sean and Dame had definitely violated by having her snatched up. He knew Dame was Ace's, but he was ready for Sean. He had imagined about a million different ways to kill him.

Elijah stopped the boys from beating the two men and ordered someone to hose them down. He wasn't sure what Ace and Darren had in store for the two men, but he knew they wanted both men to be awake and alert.

Ace stood off in the shadows smoking a cigarette. He wasn't into torture that much. He felt like Dame deserved worse than death, but he couldn't let him live after tonight. Dame always found a way to bounce back. He was cutting the head off this snake once and for all. This would be the last time Dame would come for him.

Ace went over and stood alongside Darren as they looked at the various tools and devices spread out on the table. They had everything from drills, hammers, various sizes of knives and guns, as well as surgical equipment. While it seemed like Darren would take a while to think about his plan, Ace had already decided. He picked up the surgical scalpel not sure if the blade was big enough, but he didn't care too much. He would make sure it got the job done. He grabbed the scalpel, the bottle of alcohol, and a roll of duct tape.

He strolled over to where Dame was strapped to a folding chair. Dame was in out of consciousness due to the savage beatings he had been receiving for the last few days. He'd lost a lot of blood while he was tied up. Ace poured the alcohol over his body causing him to scream out and wake up from the pain.

"AHHHHHHH!" Dame screamed out as Ace ripped the duct tape from his mouth.

Ace was pleasantly surprised at the fact that there was no fear in Dame's eyes at this very moment. He couldn't wait to wipe the smirk off of Dame's face. If he weren't so black, all of Dame's skin would be covered in bruises. Both of his eyes were swollen shut, and he was even missing a few teeth. Still, Dame was smirking at the fact that he'd gotten over on Dominic "Ace" Malone. Ace thought he was so untouchable, but Dame had touched both his daughter and *his wife*.

"So you did all this shit for what?" Ace asked. He didn't really care. Dame was going to die either way, but he felt like he should get an explanation as to why. Maybe he could even clear up some things with Dame.

"You always thought you was hot shit. You are nothing but a crooked ass cop. You thought you could come in and take what was mine. I took what was yours, *twice*." Dame said then spit blood out at Ace's feet.

"What you talking about twice? Nigga, this was the first and only time you can ever say you caught me slipping!" Ace shouted. He should have followed his first mind and offed this nigga. Dame always did talk too much.

Dame laughed before responding. "Make sure you call and tell your wife to take care of *our daughter*."

Anger quickly coursed through Ace's body as he realized what Dame was saying. He took the scalpel and cut off Dame's dick with one swipe. Blood squirted all over Ace's shirt but he didn't care. He shoved the dick in Dame's mouth to muffle his cries. Then he took duct tape and covered Dame's mouth with it. Dame began to thrash around in the chair as his air supply was cut off. His thrashing was also causing his blood to leak out faster.

"Eat a dick, nigga." Ace said and spat on Dame's dying body. He took off his shirt and threw it on the ground before walking out.

Elijah was the only one to bust out laughing. Darren looked at him like he had lost his mind. Every man in the room had unknowingly grabbed their dicks at the sight before them. Losing your dick was worse than death to a man. To actually die by choking on your own dick was some real sick shit.

"Nigga! I thought you was crazy! That nigga made him choke on his dick!" Elijah wiped the tears from his eyes. "That's an instant classic."

Darren didn't even feel like he could follow up on such an act. The rage in his body was gone. He was low-key feeling sick at what he'd just witnessed. He picked up the AK47 and opened fire at Sean's body emptying all the rounds into him, sending the chair falling over. It was a way nicer death than Sean deserved, but he didn't have it in him to torture anyone tonight. He pulled another blunt from his ear and walked out of the front door of the warehouse.

About ten minutes later, Elijah joined Darren and Ace outside. Elijah had just finished instructing the rest of the team on how to get rid of the bodies and clean the place. He was still hyped from all that had taken place, but he could sense the calm in Darren and Ace so he held it in.

"My daughters chose y'all little niggas for a reason. I been MIA for a minute, but I just want y'all to know all this foolishness ends tonight. If you can't protect my baby girls, then I'd rather you walk away now. I'm going to be around for a minute catching up with the girls. I won't hesitate to pop one of you if anything else happens to them." Ace spoke calmly.

Darren and Elijah both respected what he had to say. Darren knew he had a lot of making up to do with Kai, so he was ready to head home to her. Elijah wasn't sure what the status of he and Khloé's relationship was at the moment, but he was planning to get her back. He was giving her space for now.

They both dapped up Ace before they turned to leave.

******

The next morning Darren laid awake next to Kai. He had been up all night watching her sleep peacefully. Even with drool hanging off the corner of her mouth and her light snoring, Kai was the most beautiful woman to him. He knew one day she would be his wife. They just needed to have a serious talk about their future. Darren didn't ever want to lose her again.

"Stop watching me." Kai said wiping the side of her mouth with her hand. She could feel Darren's eyes on her as she slept.

"Don't talk to me with your morning breath." Darren teased causing Kai to pull the blanket over her face in embarrassment.

Kai got up and went to the bathroom to brush her teeth and wash her face. She loved waking up to Darren in the morning. She hoped it lasted. They hadn't talked about everything that had gone down before she was taken. She knew they needed to, but she was hoping to live in happiness for at least a few more days. Her plans were thrown out the window when she exited the bathroom and saw the serious look on Darren's face.

"I know you only been back for a minute, but we have to talk before we go any further." Darren said. He didn't want to seem like it was confrontational, he just wanted to make sure they were on the same page.

"I know I should have went about things better concerning you and Eric." Kai began. Darren's jaw clenched at the mention of his name. "I just knew no matter what, Eric would never be available to me. He is engaged to someone else. He has been a part of my life for the last two years. It was just hard to give that up and take a chance on something real. I see the way you are with the twins. You are exactly everything I ever prayed for. I lied to you only because I pray this baby is yours. I want to build a family with you."

Darren listened to her confession. It seemed genuine. He could understand where she was coming from. He knew Kai was a good girl and never wanted to be in this position. He needed her to understand that if she was choosing him then there would be no more secret meetings or phone calls with Eric.

"I get what you saying, baby girl. I just need you to understand, I know what's going on. This is not easy for any of us. I just need you to be honest and not hide things. The fact that you were keeping secrets had me feeling some type of way. You can tell me anything. I'd rather hear it from you than find out from somewhere else. Don't sneak and talk to him or set up secret meetings, just be real about it."

Kai respected where he came from. Before everything happened she had already decided that Darren was where she wanted to be. But seeing him laid out on the ground nearly bleeding to death opened her eyes a little bit. She could not at this moment commit herself to him. She was still weak for Eric. She knew what she had to do, but it wasn't going to be easy.

"I think I should stay at my condo until the baby is born. I don't know for certain who the father is. As much as I don't want it to be Eric's, there is still a possibility it's his. I won't contact him until the day the baby is born, if it makes you feel better. I just need to take this time to fully heal myself from that relationship before I jump in anything with you and the baby comes." Kai was scared to look in Darren's eyes. She could feel his body tense up. She knew he wasn't happy with her decision, but he had to respect it.

"Just be prepared for me to spend almost every night with you. I can't sleep without you snoring in my ear." Darren joked.

Kai play punched him on the arm and then kissed him. She giggled when she felt his hands pulling up the t-shirt she had slept in. She knew exactly what he wanted and she had missed him. She got up and straddled him, though. Even though he never complained, he was still not physically in the best shape. He still had stitches and she didn't need any of them busting open.

Chapter 11

"Are you sure that's what you want to do?" Her lawyer asked her.

"Yeah, it will all work out don't worry." Olivia said placing the $5,000 cash on his desk. It was too easy to bribe people with money these days.

"Well I'll have the papers drawn up and sent off." Her lawyer said shaking her hand and walking her out of his office.

Olivia smiled as she rode the elevator down to the parking lot. Who did Ace think he was divorcing her? He had no reason. She had been a damn good wife to him. Even when he was out running the streets and chasing after other women, she'd stayed faithful and continued to keep house and raise their children. He gave no excuse as to why he was seeking the divorce in the first place. "Irreconcilable differences" was very vague. She had tried to call him several times but got no response. If it wasn't about the twins, Ace was not interested in anything Olivia had to say.

Just as she sat in her car, her phone rang. She frantically searched through her purse for the phone hoping it was Ace and that he'd changed his mind. She would go back upstairs and cancel everything. To her dismay, it was Dame calling for the third time that day. She was glad Ace was across the country and her nanny was doing such a good job with the twins. If Ace found out she was going behind his back sleeping with his old partner, he'd flip. Nonetheless, she answered the phone.

"Hey." Olivia answered cheerfully.

"I'm at our spot waiting on you. When you coming by?" Dame replied.

It had been a month since they had hooked up and Olivia had been dodging him. The second time they had hooked up was right around the time Ace started tripping on her. She knew there was no way Ace had found out about her sleeping with Dame. Dame always paid cash for the hotel and they always arrived and left separately. She was very careful.

"I don't know." Olivia hesitated. She really wanted her family back and sleeping with Dame was going to cause more harm than good.

"Come on. I got some candy." Dame said as he did a line for her to hear.

Olivia's panties got wet thinking about it. Sex with Dame was good, but with the coke, it was explosive. She gave in and told him she was on her way before hanging up. She called the nanny and made sure the twins were good. She also let her know that she wouldn't be home until the following morning, then made her way to the hotel.

Olivia had been calling Dame for about a week straight and hadn't gotten one call back. His line just went straight to voicemail as she had filled his inbox up with too many messages. She needed an update on their plans with Ace. Dame was supposed to have caught up with him by now. It seemed like Dame was dragging his feet. She was ready to take matters into her own hands. She was ready to show Ace he wasn't as untouchable as he thought he was.

"Four bodies found in Conyers home.... Gas line may have been tampered with. Rockdale County Police suspect foul play. More tonight on WSB-TV News at 5."

Olivia froze in place watching the news story unfold before her. She couldn't tell if the house was Dame's safe house or not. Just as the thought crossed her mind, it left. The news anchor recited the exact address confirming it was the same house. She now knew why Dame wasn't answering her calls; he was dead.

Olivia paced back and forth in her hotel room wondering if it would be smart to make this call. Should she just leave well enough alone and return home to her husband in New York. She picked up her Samsung Galaxy S6 and scrolled down to Ace's name. She went back and forth for a few more moments trying to calm her nerves, so she wouldn't sound so distraught. She was certain Ace had something to do with the explosion at the safe house, but she needed to know for sure that one of the bodies found didn't belong to her daughter. She hit the name on her cell to place the call.

"What the fuck you calling me for? Wait til I catch up with you, stupid bitch." Ace answered on the third ring.

"Hey *husband.* Not happy to hear from me?" Olivia laughed. Pissing off Ace brought some joy to her sad life.

"What you want, O? I don't have time for your bullshit today."

"I'm going to be in LA for about a week. I wanted to see if you wanted to hook up for old times' sake." She lied.

"Ask me what you really want to know." Ace said getting angrier. He didn't have time to play games with Olivia. She knew exactly the bullshit she was involved in and what it would cost her.

"You have her?"

"Yep."

"I didn't—" She started to say, but realized he had already hung up on her.

Olivia was furious. There was a time when Ace would stop everything and cater to her every need. They had gotten engaged only two months after knowing each other and pregnant soon after. He had swept her off of her feet with expensive jewelry, gifts, and trips. He would do any and every thing she asked of him without any hesitation. The last few times they had met up over the years, he had shown nothing but disgust at the sight of her. He was the one who had abandoned their family, but he was treating her like she had done something wrong. There was no way he could think she had something to do with Dame's plan to kidnap their daughter.

Sure she had wanted revenge, but would never bring harm to her own child or grandchild. The fact that Kai knew she was there didn't look good on her part, but they had it all wrong. She wasn't going to let any harm come to her. She just needed to keep her there, so Dame wouldn't think she was going to cross him. Olivia was so caught up in her own plans for Ace, she had forgotten to protect her own child.

There was only one other reason Ace could be so angry with her, but she knew there was no way he could have found out her secret. She had done everything in her power to keep it hidden from him. Unless someone had crossed her… She shook that thought from her head. In order for them to cross her, they'd have to put themselves on the line as well. She knew that couldn't be it. She was just being silly.

Olivia got up from the bed and began throwing her clothes in her suitcase. She knew it would only be a matter of time before Ace came for her. Seeing what he did to Dame, she didn't want to feel Ace's wrath. She called down to the front desk and let them know she would be checking out. She called up her husband, Gregg, and let him know that she'd be home soon. She hoped that hiding in plain sight would work to her advantage if Ace came looking for her.

She called and booked a trip back to New York to be with her husband. She needed to lay low for a while. She would be back soon and Ace would finally see how much he fucked up by abandoning her.

Chapter 12

Khloé was happy to have her twin back home, but she was ready for Kai and Ace to leave the condo. Kai had been moping around the house for the last month and a half, because she really wanted to be with Darren, but had chosen to live in the condo until the baby was born. Ace was being too overbearing. He was constantly in their business and wanted to know their every move. Khloé and Kai had been living on their own for so long, they were having a hard time adjusting to the parenting. They missed their father while he was gone, but it was time for them to get back to their lives, and he was doing too much.

"We need to talk." Khloé said sitting on the edge of Kai's bed as she watched her twin try on clothes for her date with Darren.

"What's up, Khloé?" Kai asked without turning around. None of her clothes were fitting, even the maternity clothes she'd recently purchased. Her 6 month pregnant belly was sticking out in everything.

"Not to be mean. I mean, I missed you a whole lot, but when are you going home?" Khloé asked trying to be gentle. Being pregnant had Kai's emotions all over the place. The last thing she wanted to do was make her twin cry.

"I am home." Kai asked turning to give Khloé the screw face.

"I mean to your house… with Darren?" Khloé said looking down at the red area carpet. She wasn't trying to start a fight. She could just tell that's where Kai wanted to be anyways.

"We decided to wait until the baby comes. If the baby is his, then I will move in with him." Kai said deciding on a black maxi dress. Picking up her black Michael Kors sandals with the gold MK logo, she put her outfit on the bed and began fixing her hair.

"But you miss him. If the baby's not his, then what are you guys going to do?"

"We're still going to be together. We will just figure out the rest when the time comes."

"What about Eric?"

"I blocked his number for now. When I give birth, Darren and I will do the paternity test. If it's Eric's, I will call. If it's not, I never have to speak to him again." Kai said like she had it all figured out.

Khloé still had a lot more questions, but she knew how Kai hated to be bothered with too many questions at one time. For now, she would just swallow her opinions and continue to watch Kai go crazy from being away from Darren.

"Now what are we going to do about dad?" Kai asked trying to slide her swollen feet into her sandals.

"I know!" Khloé laughed. It was like Kai had read her mind. They could feel each other's emotions sometimes. She knew that Kai was equally tired of their father. Khloé had warmed up to Ace a little, but Kai was still harboring abandonment issues when it came to their parents. It would take some time for her to forgive Ace.

"You need to tell him it's time for him to go back to his other family or wherever he was hiding." Kai checked her hair in the mirror. She was thinking about changing the color. Red was a lot of maintenance and with a new baby on the way, she wasn't sure she could maintain it. Maybe she'd return to her natural dirty blonde/sandy brown color. She made a note to hit up Ivy for an appointment.

"Why me?" Khloé asked with a confused look.

"Aren't you all daddy's girl with him now? It's time for him to go."

"Whatever, Kai. I just don't want to hurt his feelings." Khloé stood up for their father. Kai needed to get over whatever ill feelings she was carrying. Ace was trying to make an effort. He had told them why he left them and stayed away for so long. Khloé nor Kai liked it, but they had to accept the fact that he felt like what he was doing was in their best interest and move on. Khloé knew it was easier said than done. "Don't forget he saved your life."

"Bye, Khloé." Kai ended the conversation by walking into her bathroom and closing the door.

Khloé took the hint and went to find Ace. She wasn't sure exactly how to go about bringing up the subject. She didn't want him to feel like they were kicking him out, especially since he helped pay the bills, but it was past time for him to go. She found him in the kitchen looking for food, as always. He ate up everything in the house and couldn't cook for nothing. Khloé couldn't count how many times he had burned something on the stove. He rarely went to the grocery store to replace anything he'd eaten.

"What's up, baby doll?" He asked stuffing Kai's frozen grapes into his mouth.

"You know she's going to get you for eating her grapes." Khloé laughed. Kai didn't play about her food. Pregnancy had her greedy. She didn't even share with Darren when he was over.

"I'm going to buy her some before she notices." Ace said offering the container to Khloé.

"You? Go to the grocery store. Yeah right." Khloé laughed.

Ace didn't like the way she laughed. He felt like he was being helpful by being there. He also felt like they were growing closer. Khloé was clearly holding something back. Before he could say something, she spoke up.

"We need to talk, Dad." Khloé said getting serious. "We love having you here—"

"Speak for yourself." Kai said grabbing the container of grapes from their father and then leaving out of the front door. "Bye."

"She does too. She just doesn't have any feelings." Khloé said half joking. "We are just used to having our own place and you being here is awkward for everyone. Don't you have some things to get back to in California?"

"Not really. I haven't worked a case in about 5 years. But I can start looking for something more permanent here in Atlanta. Will that be okay? I'd like to be around for my grandson." Ace suggested. His eyes sparkled at thoughts of him becoming a grandpa. The day he found out Kai was having a boy was one of the best days of his life. He always wanted a son, but had been blessed with the twins. He never had any children after he and Olivia split.

"That would be good. We can always hang out and you can come over, but we all need a little more time to get used to being a family." Khloé was glad he understood. She wasn't trying to hurt him. She too was excited about having a nephew. She couldn't wait to spoil him. She grabbed her keys to leave out as well. "Oh by the way. Stop telling Elijah where I'm at."

"You don't want to be with him, but that don't stop you from driving that car." Ace observed. He thought Elijah and Khloé made a good couple. Elijah reminded him a lot of himself. Ace was once young and wildin' in the streets, but he was very serious about Olivia. He knew she was wifey the first time he laid eyes on her. It just took him a minute to settle down and be the family man she needed. When the twins were born, he finally understood and apologized for all the women and heart breaks. He thought she was the one, but he had been very wrong. He didn't want his daughter to settle for the wrong person either, but he could tell Elijah loved her.

Khloé shook her head at her father as he went back in the fridge for more food. She got ready to head to the mall to meet Malik. Khloé stuck her tongue out at Ace and left. She didn't have a comeback other than she loved that car.

Chapter 13

"Damn, bae." Darren moaned as Kai went down on him. She was attempting to suck the skin off his dick. She had learned to take his 9 inches all the way down her throat without gagging. He could feel the saliva dripping down onto his balls, her mouth was so wet. She pulled him from her mouth and used her spit to stroke his dick while she took one of his balls into her mouth and sucked before moving onto the next one.

Darren felt like he was about to bust and didn't want to do it so soon. He wanted to get all up in her guts. He grabbed her hair and pulled her up. He kissed her lips before turning her around and bending her over the bed. He gave her ass a loud smack before diving into her juicy center with his tongue. He licked and slurped causing her juices to leak down her thighs and his chin.

"Yesssssss. Mmmm." Kai moaned as his fingers massaged her clit. Darren was a pro at eating the box. She couldn't take what he was giving her. She started to run, but he grabbed onto her legs and pulled her back. Her legs started to tremble as she came all over his face. It had been months since she last had his sex, she wasn't sure she could hang.

Darren stood and wiped her juices off his mouth with the back of his hand. He smacked her ass one more time before spreading her cheeks. He rubbed the head of his dick up and down her clit feeling how wet and gushy she was. He slowly slid all of him into her causing Kai to moan out.

"Ummmm." Kai moaned as she slowly began to throw it back on him. He filled her so perfectly. He not only had length, but his dick was thick as hell. It was like he was sculpted completely for her. His slow pace was teasing her and she wanted more. She began pushing back on him.

"That's it, ma. Throw that ass back." Darren coached her.

Kai sped up her pace a little. She could feel another orgasm building up inside her. She worked her hips in a circle. Darren gripped her ass cheeks to slow down her pace. Kai liked to be in control, but he wasn't having that tonight. He wanted to give her long, slow, deep strokes. He sucked the tip of his thumb and applied pressure to her back door.

Kai wanted to cry. Between the pace Darren was going and the pressure at her other hole, she wasn't sure she could hold on. She could feel him deep in her stomach. He pushed down on her spot with every stroke. The way he knew her body was driving her insane. She had been with others before, but they didn't come close to her man. Darren made love to her body and soul.

"Ahhh! I'm cumming!" She screamed out as her legs gave out underneath her and she began squeezing his dick with her walls.

Darren caught her before she could fall on her pregnant stomach. He sped up his strokes while her muscles contracted around him. The feeling was too good. He could hear her juices sloshing around as he drove into her harder and deeper. He wanted her to come once more when he did. Her essence ran out like a faucet over his shaft and balls. Whoever said pregnant pussy was the best, never lied. A couple of strokes later, he was nutting up inside of her causing her to cum again.

After their orgasms subsided, he laid down on the bed. She climbed on top of him straddling his body. He smirked up at her knowing what she was about to do. His dick rocking up at the thought of another round. "Come ride your dick, baby."

Kai eased down on it and rode him until they both came once more.

******

The next morning Kai woke up to the smell of pancakes and bacon. She did a happy dance on the way to the bathroom to brush her teeth. Darren knew exactly how to wake a girl up. When she returned from the bathroom, he was seated on the bed eating his plate. On a tray there was another plate that held pancakes, scrambled eggs with cheese and tomatoes, bacon, home fried potatoes, cheese grits with a spoon of grape jelly, toast, and orange juice. Kai was amazed. This is exactly what she told him she wanted before they fell asleep last night.

"You fixed all this?" She asked Darren who was digging into his food.

"Nah. Ms. Pam is downstairs." Darren admitted then smirked. He should have taken the credit. That would have gotten him a repeat of last night.

Kai dug into her food and cleared her plate in under 5 minutes. Darren laughed at how greedy she had become, but she didn't care. She and the baby were serious about eating. They didn't want anyone playing with their meals. Darren had gotten scolded more than once for making her wait to eat.

"So what you got planned for today, greedy?" Darren asked. He hated that she didn't want to move back in with him after she was rescued from Dame. He felt like the baby she was carrying was his and there was no reason for her not to be home with him and the twins where she belonged. He wanted to respect her wished but at the same time, he wanted to go to her condo, pack all her shit, and bring her home.

"A little baby shopping and then a pedicure." Kai said adjusting the pillows behind her head. "After my nap."

He smiled at her needing a nap. They had just woke up and all she did was eat, but was claiming to be tired. "I'll go with you. We need to discuss names and a few other things anyways."

"Names?" Kai hadn't thought about baby names. She wasn't sure who the father of her baby was and felt like that right should be given to that person only.

"Yeah. I already got a junior, so I was thinking about other names that start with a D. So far I like Desmond or Derrick." Darren continued. He could sense her hesitation. He knew the possibility of the baby not being his, but he didn't care. He felt like it was going to be his.

"Derrick. That's cute, I guess." Kai said turning to her side. She could never find a comfortable position with her pregnant belly always getting in the way. She let out an appreciative sigh as Darren wrapped his arms around her and began rubbing her stomach. The baby started kicking wildly. She laughed before turning back on her back.

"See, he knows daddy." Darren said and began talking baby talk to her stomach.

Kai could see the excitement in Darren's eyes as he bonded with what she hoped would be his son. She hadn't thought about Eric in a while, but it wasn't fair that he would miss out on moments like this if it turned out to be his baby. The tears started flowing before she could even fight it. She hated all the emotions that came along with being pregnant. One minute she could be happy and laughing and the next, she'd just burst out in tears.

Darren was confused on what to do. They were having a good moment, so he felt. He didn't know if he was the cause of her tears or not, but he hated to see her cry. He stood up and walked around the edge of the bed. Sitting next to her, he pulled her to his chest and let her cry.

"I never wanted to be this girl. I don't even know who my baby's father is." She cried into his chest.

There was nothing Darren could say. It was a bad spot for anyone to be in. He knew she never intended to get pregnant that way, so he said nothing. As far as Eric went, he just hoped the nigga was smart enough to keep his distance like he'd been doing. Darren wouldn't hesitate to beat his bougie ass again. He heard Kai's light snoring and knew she'd cried herself to sleep. He slid from under her then covered her with the blanket. He left the room to go play with the twins some while Kai slept.

Chapter 14

Justice had been calling Elijah to bring EJ home for a week straight. Even though Justice had initially hid her pregnancy and baby from Elijah, no one could say that she wasn't a good mother. EJ was smart for his age. She spent a lot of time working with him. Since she wasn't working, he filled most of her days with something to do. They would read stories and watch movies. Sometimes, she'd take him out to different places around the city. Without him, she was going crazy just sitting around.

The only good thing about EJ being with his father was that she knew Elijah was alone. She knew that Elijah would never bring some random girl around their son. The only female she had to worry about was that Khloé girl. The way Elijah spoke of her let Justice know Elijah actually had feelings for Khloé. Just the thought of Elijah ending up with some other girl after all this time, had Justice's blood boiling.

She had gotten a warning from the doctor to keep her blood pressure down. On her last appointment the doctor had informed her that not only was her pressure sky high, but her baby was underweight and underdeveloped. He felt like there was a 25% chance the baby would come out with some form of disability.

Justice had tried to tell Elijah how high risk her pregnancy was, but all he did was tell her she needed to start taking it easy. She told him that he was stressing her out and causing her pressure to be high. He just said she needed to chill out. He wasn't her man, so she shouldn't even be stressing over him.

Justice refused to believe Elijah was done with her. She fell in love with him when she was just 14 years old. He was her first everything. How could he just throw away so many years of history over one mistake she made? She had stayed with him through all the lies, drugs, and cheating. He couldn't even look past her hiding EJ even though she had good reasons. If she wasn't sure he'd just run to that Khloé girl, she would take EJ and return to New York with this baby too.

Suddenly, she felt a tightening in her stomach followed by a shooting pain. Something was wrong. Once again she tried to dial Elijah's number, but he sent her call to voicemail. "Eli! Something's wrong with the baby! I'm having contractions! It's too early!" She cried into his voicemail.

She tried to get off her bed, but another contraction ripped through her body. She was only six months pregnant. She knew what labor felt like and she was definitely experiencing it. With Elijah not answering and no friends or family nearby, she had no choice but to call 911. After giving the operator her address and saying what was wrong, she tried to move towards downstairs to open the front door so the paramedics wouldn't kick it in. She cursed herself for begging

Elijah for this big ass house. She edged her way to the end of the bed and when she stood, she could see all the blood on the bed comforter and feel it soaking through her leggings.

Justice took slow breaths and walked slowly towards her bedroom door. She made it down the stairs and to the front door. She managed to unlock and open it right before she passed out.

******

"Dang, bae. Who blowing up your phone like that?" Bria asked Elijah as he took his turn swinging the baseball bat. This was only their second actual date, and she could actually admit she was starting to like Elijah. He always did things outside the box. He didn't just take her somewhere like Friday's and expect to hit afterwards. He had been showing her a lot of new things. Like now, they were at the batting cages drinking beer and having so much fun.

"Probably my worrisome ass baby mama. That chick won't take the hint that I'm done with her ass." Elijah said swinging and hitting the ball. Bria watched as each muscle in his toned arms flexed with every movement his body made. His chocolate skin was glistening with sweat. She couldn't wait to have those strong arms wrapped around her later.

Elijah looked back at Bria. He smirked. He could tell she was eye fucking him. The way she bit her bottom lip was the sexiest sight he'd ever seen. He had met her inside Greenbriar

Mall, a hood chick's favorite spot, located on the west side of Atlanta. She was walking ahead of him and all he could focus on was the way her ass jiggled inside her leggings. It's like each cheek had a mind of its own, but they still worked beautifully together.

Bria was 5'2 with smooth light brown skin and almond shaped grey eyes. She had thick plump lips that did wonders when they were wrapped around his 11 inches. Her hair was in a long weave that was straight and went down to the middle of her back. Her breasts were tiny, but she more than made up for it with her small waist and fat ass.

"This is like the fourth time she called, you sure you don't want to answer? It could be something with your son." Bria suggested.

"Nah, my son is with my assistant right now. He's straight." Elijah couldn't care less about what dramatic episode Justice was trying to pull today. She had been following him around, leaving him crazy voicemails, and even going as far as to sit outside his house at night. "You want to go again… Even though you suck?"

"I do not suck!" Bria giggled. She had taken her turn and hadn't hit a single ball, even with Elijah standing there holding the bat with her. Elijah gave her a look that said yeah right. He was about to say something when he noticed his phone light up again. This time it was Jazzy calling so he picked up.

"What's up? Everything straight?" Elijah answered.

"EJ is good, but Justice—" Jazzy started to say but was cut off. She wasn't really sure how to tell Elijah.

"I don't want to hear it. That girl thinks because she is having my baby, I'm supposed to jump whenever she calls. She got me fucked up." The last thing Elijah wanted to talk about was Justice right now.

"Well… She had the nurse call from the hospital when she couldn't reach you. She, um… She lost the baby."

"Fuck!" Elijah ran his hands down his face. He had fucked up by ignoring her. He felt like shit. He put a $100 bill on the table to cover their food, drinks, and play time and rushed out of the door with Bria on his heels. He didn't have time to drop her off at home so she'd just have to come with him.

He figured Justice was at Piedmont Hospital since it was the closest one to her home. He did about 90 on I-75 headed towards downtown Atlanta. She had told him that she was having a hard pregnancy. The doctor told him that she was high risk. He just thought she was trying to get him to feel sorry for her and come around more. If he'd taken the time and listened to her or gone to an appointment, none of this would have happened.

Bria sat silently on the passenger side as Elijah sped down the interstate. She could sense something was wrong, but Elijah hadn't told her exactly what was going on. She decided to check her phone instead. She had been trying to get in contact with her dad for a while, but he hadn't returned one call. She figured he didn't get good cell reception out where he was. She made a note to go out to see if everything was still good on his end.

Twenty minutes later, Elijah pulled up in the parking garage and turned the engine off. He sat for a moment and thought about what he would say to Justice. He wasn't thrilled about having another baby with her, but it was still a part of him that was gone. He wasn't as attached because he wasn't carrying the child inside him, but a loss is still a loss. He ran his hand over his head and let out a frustrated breath.

Bria reached over and rubbed his shoulder in an attempt to comfort him. She had no idea who was in the hospital, but she could already tell it wasn't good news. Elijah had gone from playful at the fun park to distraught in less than thirty minutes. She considered maybe calling an Uber to take her home since she didn't want to intrude on this serious moment.

Elijah finally gathered himself and got out of the car. He walked in the hospital pulling Bria behind him. He asked the nurse for Justice's room and headed in that direction. Each step he took his feet got heavier and heavier as they approached her door.

Elijah and Bria stood outside the door for a moment. He was hesitant to go in, but Bria knew she should stay outside the room. She took a seat in the chair next to the door. Elijah peeked in the room and saw Justice sitting up in the bed staring blankly out of the window. Seeing the obvious pain in her expression, he wasn't sure if he could comfort her. He took in a long breath and exhaled before walking into her room.

Justice didn't even move when she felt him sit on the edge of her bed. She had no words for him. She had been calling him all day. He couldn't even answer the phone when she needed him most. If he could have acted like he cared and not stressed her out the entire pregnancy, none of this would have happened.

"Jus, you need anything," Elijah asked. He really didn't know what to do, but he felt like he should be doing something. Whatever she wanted, he would make sure she got it.

"Where's my son, Elijah?" Justice asked without turning to face him. She couldn't bear to look into his eyes.

"He's with Jazzy. You want me to have her bring him up here?" Elijah was looking for a reason to leave out of the room. His heart broke watching her. He'd never be with her again, but he still had mad love for her.

"So he wasn't even with you while I was in my house bleeding out from losing *my* child?" Justice shouted. "Where were you huh, Elijah? Probably out with some hoe, ignoring my phone calls. I laid there dialing your number over and over. I refused to do anything until you got here. I had to push *my* baby out and it was already dead!"

Justice broke down crying. She couldn't believe him. The whole time she was laying in the hospital, she was thinking he was busy with EJ and that's why he hadn't bothered to answer. The fact that her child was safe at home with his father had provided her a sense of comfort. But no, the guilty look on his face said it all. He had pawned her baby off on someone else so he could go out tricking off with some hoe. She looked at his handsome face once more. Though she could see the concern and hurt, she couldn't bring herself to care.

"Get the fuck out! Bring me my son! I don't need your bullshit anymore! This is the last time you will treat me like I ain't shit." Justice was hysterical at this point. She wanted Elijah out of her presence and away from her.

"Jus, I—" Elijah started to say.

"I don't give a fuck what you have to say. Get the fuck out and don't come back until you have my son! Matter fact, just have Jazzy bring him."

Elijah got up and walked over to Justice. He held her as she broke down in his arms. Her heart was literally broken. There were no words that could be said to take away or describe the way she felt from losing her child. Elijah had only further pushed the knife in her chest by not being there for her when she needed him the most.

"Hey Eli, I'm going to call a cab. I'll talk to you later. Sorry about your loss." Bria popped into the room to let Elijah know she was leaving. She had been listening to their entire conversation. She was waiting for the perfect moment to pop in. She could have just texted him, but she had wanted to stir up drama between him and Justice.

"What the fuck?" Justice pushed Elijah away. "You brought your hoe up here with you?"

"I ain't no hoe and you going to stop calling me one." Bria said with her hands on her hip.

"You's a hoe. You already knew this nigga was in a relationship with some bitch and he was having a baby with me?" She waited for Bria to respond. When she noticed the look of guilt spread across Bria's face, she continued. "You still stuck around so that makes you a hoe."

Justice was taking her anger out on Bria. She didn't give a damn anymore. She had just lost her child and Elijah was being hella disrespectful by bringing this girl up to the hospital. Anybody could get it right now. Bria started towards the bed like she was about to do something, but Elijah pushed her back outside the door.

"What the fuck, yo! She just lost my baby and you going to try and fight her? I ain't about to let that shit go down. You got to go, ma."

"She the one started with me! I ain't no hoe!" Bria rolled her eyes and smacked her lips.

"Yeah, but she hurting. Get your mind right. I might holla at you later." Elijah said turning back to go to Justice. He didn't have shit else to say to Bria after the way she had just acted. He thought she was cool, but he was wrong. He just saw a side of her that he didn't like or respect.

Chapter 15

Justice lay staring out the window of her hospital room at nothing in particular. Elijah had hurt her to her core by bringing that girl up to her hospital room. That moment should have just remained between the two of them, but he made it worse for her by showing he didn't care about her feelings at all. After kicking the girl out of the room, Justice still couldn't bear to look at Elijah.

"You can wait for Jazzy in the waiting room. Bring me my son when she gets here." Justice dismissed him without ever turning her head to look at him.

"Justice, I'm sorry. When I got the call, I wasn't thinking. I just got up here as fast as I could. I never wanted any of that to happen." Elijah apologized. He didn't think Bria would cause a scene like that. If anything she should have been more sympathetic to Justice's situation since she was a woman. Elijah knew he was wrong. He would apologize a million times if it would wipe the depressed look off Justice's face.

Contrary to what everyone believed, Elijah loved Justice. She was the first girl he ever loved. She was the only one not affected by his handsome looks or wealth. She always told him the truth no matter how much it hurt him. She never put up with his foolishness. This new Justice that was vindictive and conniving, he didn't know her.

When Justice first caught him in that apartment with that random girl and disappeared, he was heartbroken. He couldn't handle the fact that he'd hurt her so badly that she wanted nothing to do with him. He searched high and low looking for her. He sat outside her mother's old brownstone in Brooklyn for a week straight waiting on Justice to show up, but she never did. He would call her cell phone even though he was sure she had blocked his number, just to hear her voice. When they were younger, Justice was the only one who could calm him when he was going through one of his hard times dealing with his mother.

He looked at her now and couldn't believe this is what he'd turned her into. Without arguing with her, he turned and walked to the waiting room. He sat in a chair with his head against the wall and waited for Jazzy to show up with EJ. He planned to go in and let Justice know he was taking EJ home, so she could get some rest.

"Why you out here?" Jazzy said rushing into the waiting room. She could see the hurt on her boss's face. She knew Justice had lost the baby. Elijah should be in there comforting her. She hoped he didn't do anything stupid while that girl was laid up in the hospital. By the look on his face, she could see that's exactly what he'd done.

"I fucked up." Elijah said shaking his head. He couldn't retell the story of what had gone down with Bria. It was too embarrassing and there was no excuse for it.

"Well go in there and fix it." Jazzy handed EJ to Elijah. She then went in the room to express her condolences to Justice. She stayed in the room for a few minutes talking with Justice before she came out. She gave Elijah a hateful glare before walking to the elevator to leave.

"Pray for me, little man." Elijah said to a sleeping EJ.

"Give me my baby." Justice said reaching for EJ.

"You should get some rest tonight. They should be letting you go tomorrow. I'll just keep EJ until you're ready to get around." Elijah said trying to throw out a peace offering.

"So you can hand him off to your assistant while you run around Atlanta with your little hoes. No thanks. I'll *keep my* child." Justice said. She stood and laid EJ down in the hospital bed, so she could change into the scrub bottoms one of the nurses had thankfully given her. The room was cold and her clothes had been thrown out from the amount of blood on them.

Elijah didn't know what to do. He grabbed her and hugged her tightly to his chest. He gave her a kiss on the forehead before letting her go and walking out of her room. He granted her wishes for now, but he would be sure to check on her tomorrow night. She wasn't going to push him away like that. They'd both lost a child and neither of them were fine. He headed to Bria's house to confront her about the bullshit scene she caused earlier.

The next morning Justice grabbed her discharge papers off the tray next to her bed and walked out of the room. She had called her mother, who now lived in Virginia, and made plans to stay with her a while. She was making a quick stop at her house for a few things then going straight to the airport and leaving on the first plane out. She had to get away from Atlanta and Elijah. No good had come for her by being here. She hated to take EJ away from his father, but she needed him with her. Having just lost a child, she needed EJ by her side at all times.

******

"NOOOOOOO!" Bria cried out, causing Elijah to jump up from his sleep. He had come over to cuss her ass out after the whole hospital incident. Needless to say they smashed and ended up falling asleep together.

He blinked a few times to adjust to the light in the room before looking towards Bria. She held her phone tightly clutched to her chest as she broke down sitting on the edge of the bed. Elijah wasn't sure what to do, so he just sat and waited while she cried. After a few moments he went and wrapped his arms around her. She turned and cried into his chest.

Bria tried to calm herself down, but her heart was literally broken. She was not expecting the call she had just received. Her father's remains had finally been identified after two months of being in the morgue. They also had the body of her brother at a funeral home. They'd been trying to contact her family for a month. She knew her brother's mother was always away on some vacation or the other, and had no way of contacting her. She had been trying to call her father for a month. She had been working hard on something for him, and he hadn't responded to any of her calls. She had been feeling like something was wrong for about a week now, but had no idea this would be the news she'd receive.

"What happened?" Elijah asked after a few moments. Her cries had gone from hysterical to calm.

"They said… my dad… my brother…" Bria began to cry again. She couldn't even form the words, they hurt too badly. "I need to call my mother."

Elijah still didn't know what was happening as he watched her walk out of the bedroom. He hadn't meant to fall asleep at her house last night. He wanted to be there for whatever she was going through, but right now he needed to get up and hit the streets. He had just gotten a text that something foul was going on with his squad. The last few weeks, his count had been coming up short. It had been years since he had to make his presence known, but obviously people had him fucked up. He was buckling up his pants when Bria finally emerged in the doorway.

"You're leaving?" She asked somberly as she climbed into her bed. She didn't really feel like talking about the news she had just received, but she did want to be wrapped up in Elijah's strong arms.

"Yeah. I got some shit to handle. You need anything before I go?" He asked not really wanting to stay. Bria was cool, but he wasn't trying to send her signals like he wanted to be her man.

"Nah. I'm good." She pouted and laid down making sure to not look him in the face.

"Aight then, ma. I'll lock the bottom lock on the way out." Elijah turned and left.

Bria screamed into her pillow as she heard her front door close. She got up and walked to the window and watched as he pulled out of her driveway. This whole time she had been falling for him and not really focusing on what her father wanted her to do. Now she was regretting taking so long to get the job done. Her father was gone and she wouldn't rest until she found out what happened to him. She didn't feel anything at the fact that her brother was gone. Jesse was such a fuck up anyways.

Chapter 16

"So you gon' come to Sunday dinner? I want you to meet my mom and sister." Malik asked for the second time. He had been trying to hold a conversation with Khloé for the last ten minutes but she seemed preoccupied.

Khloé was unsure of what to say. She was glad since they were on the phone Malik couldn't see the hesitation and annoyance written all over her face. She had been hanging out with Malik for a few months now, but she didn't know if she wanted to meet his mother. Clearly they were not on the same path. She just saw them as friends. If she went and met his mother, he'd probably want to meet her father and sister as well. Ace and Kai were both still Team Elijah and probably would not be nice or accepting.

"Um… You don't think it's too soon?" Khloé asked.

"We been dating for a couple months, and I'm ready to make this shit official, shawty. I talked to my mom about you and she invited you to dinner. She said you sound like a nice young lady."

"I have to think about all that."

Khloé liked Malik a lot, but she was still not over Elijah. She hadn't spoken with Elijah in about a few weeks, but she laid in bed thinking about him every night still, wondering if he was with his baby-mama or some other girl. Kai told her to man up and just call him, but she felt like he was the one that was supposed to be making the effort.

"Well even if you not ready to make shit official, still come by the house. My mom can throw down in the kitchen." Malik joked after a long awkward silence.

"I can do that." Khloé reluctantly agreed. "I'll talk to you before Sunday to let you know."

"Bet." Malik said then they hung up.

Khloé got up from her bed and went to Kai's room to see if she was home. More and more Kai had been staying at Darren's, even though she still claimed she wasn't ready to move in with him. Khloé thought their relationship was cute. She was glad her sister had finally found someone. The only thing she missed about Kai being gone all the time was that they didn't hang out so much anymore. Even when Kai was on the road doing modeling jobs, they were inseparable. They pretty much kept to themselves and considered each other their best friend. Now that Kai was about to be a mother and Khloé was going to be preoccupied with Pharmacy school, they were going to have to make more of an effort to spend time together.

Khloé came up with a fun idea. She called up Ivy and Jazzy and invited them over for girls' night. Jazzy was easy to convince and said she'd stop by. Khloé had a hard time with Ivy. True to Ivy fashion, he needed a good reason to cancel his plans to come hang out with a square, a whore, and a pregnant bitch, as he put it. Khloé fought back her laughter and promised him free food and drinks. He instantly agreed. She also told him to bring his hair stuff. She needed her hair touched up and knew that Kai wanted to go back blonde before the baby came.

Right when Khloé went to knock on the door, she heard Kai talking quietly to someone on the phone.

"No. I could lose everything just sharing that little bit with you… No, you can't come to the hospital… I'm sorry… No… I can't…" Even listening to the one sided conversation, Khloé could tell that Kai was talking to Eric. Khloé knew how angry Darren got the last time he found out Kai was dealing with Eric behind his back. She didn't understand why Kai would want to ruin such a good thing with Darren, especially since Kai had set up the rules for their new arrangement. She knocked softly on the door then waited for Kai to tell her to come in.

"Come in." Kai said.

"Guess what we're doing tonight?" Khloé said excitedly. She decided not to mention the conversation she had overhead a moment ago. Kai would tell her what's going on when the time is right, she hoped.

"No, Khloé. I don't want to go out." Kai pouted. Being pregnant and in the club was not a good look. She had made fun of many girls for doing it, and she refused to become one of them.

"Good. Because Jazzy and Ivy are on the way over. We are going to have ourselves a little girls' night. Get our hair done, eat, watch movies, dance, and gossip. Just me, you, Jazzy, and Ivy." Khloé waited for Kai's reaction.

"Oooh. That sounds fun. Tell Jazzy to bring stuff to make her nachos. I've been wanting some since forever." Kai said rubbing her stomach. Just thinking about the nachos had her mouth watering.

"Okay, big mama." Khloé laughed and left out of the room to get everything ready.

******

"Now we already know Miss Khloé needs to dust the cobwebs off that thang and give it to Mr. Elijah already. I can't stand his new bitch. I don't know why he be bringing her all around and shit. She be throwing looks hunty, and you know Miss Ivy don't play that." Ivy flicked his 30" blonde wavy hair over his shoulder before continuing. "Kai's greedy pregnant ass needs to slow down before she chokes on that nacho. But I really want to know what's going on with Miss Jazzy and that fine, but weird ass nigga, Zane." Ivy said fanning himself causing all the girls to giggle.

Khloé was glad she had brought everyone together for a fun night. They were all dressed in pajamas and sitting around eating while Ivy dyed Kai's hair back to blonde. They hadn't seen Ivy since he'd done Khloé's hair for her second first date with Elijah. Jazzy had been around a lot while Kai was missing. She and Khloé had grown closer and now she was also bonding with Kai.

Ivy had already redone Khloé's highlights and wand curled Jazzy's hair. They were having a good night. Everyone was drinking, except for Kai, who was happily eating all the food and snacks they had prepared. They had Pandora playing in the background while they caught up on what's new with each other.

Jazzy blushed. She and Zane had been spending a lot of time together lately, but he hadn't made any moves yet, or expressed any interest in taking it to the next step with her. She was feeling him. He was different from any guy she had ever been with. Zane didn't talk a lot, he just did what he wanted to do. She felt if he was into her, he would have made his move already. She decided to confide in her girls to see what they thought.

"So it's like this. We been hanging out a lot lately. I've been to his house and he practically lives at mine. But we haven't done anything yet. I want to, but he stops me every time and then it just gets awkward. After first I was OK with it, but now it's been a couple months and I stopped trying." Jazzy explained.

"Now I know that fine mother fucker ain't gay!" Ivy blurted out, making Khloé and Kai throw him a look.

Kai knew all too well what it was like dating someone who wouldn't make a move on her. While she didn't feel that Zane was gay, she understood where Jazzy was coming from.

She couldn't open up and tell her exactly what had gone down with her ex, Justin, but she could offer her some advice. She could see the spark between Jazzy and Zane when they were around each other, and she felt like they had a real connection.

"You just have to tell him how you feel. Not sit down and talk, no man likes that. I mean, go over to his house, cook him his favorite meal, be naked or dress sexy, make the house so he knows exactly what you want, go all out. He won't have a choice but to either follow your lead or tell you what's up. If that fails, then hell, he may be gay 'cuz you bad, girl." Kai winked at Jazzy then laughed.

Khloé agreed. Jazzy was a beautiful girl. Standing only 5'3, she was considered plus size, but she wore her weight well with most of it being in her hips and ass. She had beautiful brown skin. Her natural hair was always done in some elegant style that looked like it took hours to do. Her confidence was always sky high, but Khloé could see that the situation with Zane had her feeling insecure.

"Let me find out Kai over there cooking dinners buck naked!" Ivy hollered.

"All the time!" Kai said confidently.

"I know that's right!" Jazzy and Ivy high-fived each other.

Khloé's face turned bright red at her sister's advice and admission. She could never do anything like that, but she had been feeling like her and Elijah needed to talk. She had heard he had a new girl he was talking to, but she wasn't going to let someone else come in and take her man. It was time for her to figure out what she wanted. Malik was cool and everything, but she compared everything he did to Elijah. She knew it was time to stop stringing Malik along and make something happen with Elijah.

"Look at Miss Khloé over here about to die. You haven't given up them goods yet?" Ivy asked sipping his Moscato like Kermit sipping some Lipton tea.

Khloé turned her head away. She was still very shy about sex. She'd had sex with Elijah quite a few times, but still considered herself very inexperienced compared to the other girls. She had barely discussed this with Kai, and now they were all looking at her waiting on an answer. With six eyes trained on her, she couldn't do anything but try to pour the tea.

"We did it." Khloé admitted shyly, the others waiting on all the details. She looked at them like they were crazy. She was not about to tell them all that.

"Ugh. You too bougie for me, Miss Khloé. I see you not trying to give up none of the dirty details so just tell us, is he packing or nah?"

"Um…" Once again all eyes were on Khloé as she thought about Ivy's question. She didn't really have anything to compare Elijah's size to, but she knew it was more than enough by the way it filled her up so deliciously. Her eyes glazed over as she unknowingly squeezed her legs together remembering the last time they were together.

"Let her live y'all." Kai quickly came to her sister's defense seeing that Khloé was hesitating with answering their questions.

"This is one lame slumber party." Ivy said. "I ain't getting no type of juicy information from you bougie, stuck up, pregnant bitches. I should have gone out. Probably could have discovered my next sugar daddy."

"You know you didn't have nothing better to do." Jazzy said laughing. Ivy was always so dramatic. He acted like he lived this fantabulous life, when really all he did was work and go home. He was serious about two things, his money and his beauty rest.

Kai turned up the music on the surround speakers in the condo just as "Cash Money Records taking over for the 9-9 and the 2000" came blaring through the speakers. All the girls and Ivy jumped up and began twerking to Juvenile's "Back that Azz Up" all over the living room.

"Kai you betta stop before you shake that baby loose." Ivy hollered. "And look at Miss Khloé, innocent my ass."

Everybody fell out laughing. This is exactly what Khloé needed, a fun night with the girls. They continued to eat, drink, and laugh the whole night.

******

Across town, the guys had met up at Elijah's townhouse to discuss their plans concerning their businesses, but conversation quickly turned to their issues with the girls. Elijah and Darren passed the blunt between each other while Zane just sat back and vibed with them.

Zane didn't smoke and rarely drank. He was kind of a health freak and spent a lot of time working on his body. He was very into technology and came across as nerdy or weird. Though he was very attractive, he was constantly misunderstood. Zane was 6 foot even with caramel colored skin. He had long, jet black, wavy hair he wore pulled into a ponytail down his back. If it weren't for his hazel eyes, people would confuse him with Lil' Fizz back in his B2K days.

"I've been trying to be nice and give Kai her space, but I'm two seconds from dragging her ass home." Darren stated. He wanted to come home to his girl every night. He had strong feelings that the baby Kai was carrying was his. Her not being with him every day was tearing him up inside. He had been there every step of the way when Camryn was pregnant with the twins. He didn't want to miss out on a moment with this baby because they were unsure of who the father was.

"Those twins got life fucked up." Elijah added. "I tried to be patient with Khloé's ass, but she running around town with some lame. She had the nerve to bring his ass up to the hospital and shit. Like what the fuck is her problem?"

Zane and Darren both looked at each other then bust out laughing. Elijah couldn't be serious. Khloé was a good girl. She wasn't used to all the drama that came along with dating someone like Elijah. He had women coming at him all over the place, a crazy baby mama, this new chick he was bringing around, and was still heavy in the streets. Zane felt like Khloé was actually smart to run the other way.

"The fuck y'all niggas laughing at?" Elijah looked between the two and then hit the blunt before passing it back to Darren.

"You had Justice running around pregnant with your second baby that you wasn't even supposed to be making. Then now you got this new piece you all around town with in the blogs and around the office. And you want Khloé to sit at home and wait for you to get your shit together? You bugging." Zane said.

"The only reason I'm with Bria is because Khloé won't get her act right." Elijah was still confused. Whenever Khloé was ready to come home, he would drop Bria and give her his full attention.

"Yo. Something is wrong with your ass." Darren said laughing. It looked like Elijah was really serious about what he was saying. He shook his head, his boy was tripping for real.

"I can't sit around with blue balls and shit waiting on her ass to get it together. Bria is fun and all, but she ain't wifey. She knows that shit." Elijah said. He had talked with Bria after the incident at the hospital with Justice and put her in her place. "Y'all all booed up and shit. I need a distraction if I can't hang with my boys."

"Booed up?" Darren asked Zane. He knew Elijah was referring to Kai and him, but he didn't know who Zane had been kicking it with lately.

"Yeah, this nigga done stole my assistant. Every time I call Jazzy's ass this nigga in the background caking her. All I hear is giggles and shit." Elijah got up to go pour himself another shot of Hennessy.

"Man, shut up. I don't be over there like that." Zane said getting defensive. He really didn't like talking about his personal life like that. He wasn't really sure what he wanted with Jazzy, but he had never really been that close with a girl either. He was at her house a lot and felt some kind of way whenever they were apart.

"Yeah, okay." Elijah and Darren laughed.

Zane reached over and mushed the side of Darren's head. Darren jumped up and squared off with Zane. Elijah watched on as they fought like some little boys. Elijah knew firsthand that Darren's hits stung like hell. They had fought many times when they were younger. He had to admit though, Zane could hold his own. He was quick and strategic with his hits. He caught Darren with a swift hit to the chin that ended the fight.

"You got that, young." Darren said and they dapped each other up. He needed to end the fight before they got to fighting for real.

"Yeah… You knew you was about to get that ass beat." Elijah laughed with Zane joining in.

"Shut up. Y'all stupid." Darren said knowing they were telling the truth.

"I been thinking. I'm ready to get my girl back now. Her 22nd is coming up. I'm about to go all out for her. You in?" Elijah asked Darren.

"Sounds good, bruh. Let's do it before my baby get here."

They sat for another hour shooting the shit and going over party ideas until they went their separate ways.

Chapter 17

"What the fuck happened?" Nyah shouted walking into her father's old house and seeing her father's longtime friend Sean's son, Jacob.

Nyah was Dame's daughter. She and Jesse had different mothers, but were both raised in the same household. Before his untimely death, Jesse had been trying to do everything in his power to upstage Nyah in their father's eyes. Nyah was the apple of Dame's eye though. Dame treated her like the son he never had. Nyah could be feminine and soft one minute then pop off and shoot someone in the head the next minute.

Jacob was as grimy as they came. He was 6'4 and had the same rich dark chocolate skin like his father. He had shoulder length dreads and ugly gold teeth with yellow diamonds. Jacob wanted to be on so bad. He did everything to look the part, but he just had no heart. He would duck and hide or send someone else to do his dirty work before he ever did anything himself.

Sean never wanted his son to enter the drug game, so he kept him away at a boarding school in a foreign country. When Jacob finished high school and college, Sean then sent him to Columbia University in New York for law school. Jacob had dropped out of Columbia Law in the first month. That was his father's dream, Jacob wanted the fast life.

Jacob only saw the glamour in what his father did. The women, the houses, the cars, and the money. He didn't know how many people his father had bodied. He didn't know that they only reason Sean stayed so close to Dame so long was that in this game you had to keep your enemies close. Sean knew Dame didn't have what it took to be the leader, but Dame had all the connections so Sean used that to his advantage and stuck around. While Dame thought he had it good with money flowing in all over Atlanta, Sean had his own operation going on up in Memphis where he was originally from.

Nyah hated Jacob with a passion. When they were younger, Jacob always felt like everything their fathers had should be handed to him because he was older and a man. Nyah worked harder at everything and actually had what it took to run the whole operation. Men twice her age looked at her with respect. She was fair, but ruthless when she had to be. She used her femininity to her advantage when necessary to get what she wanted, but didn't let anyone take advantage of her just because she was a woman.

That was more than what Jacob could say for himself. He never even bothered to take on any work. He felt like if he was paying people to work, that's exactly what they should do. What was the point of having a whole team of people, but you still had to get your hands dirty? He talked down to people and had rubbed some of their father's associates the wrong way, including Dame's connect. Between Jacob and her brother Jesse, their fathers' empire would surely fall. With Jesse out of the way, Nyah only had to deal with Jacob, and she knew exactly what to do with him. Pay him some money and send him on his way. All Jacob wanted was the money, he never had to work a day in his life for anything and would only get in her way.

"Word on the streets is some niggas from up North did it. Your brother had kidnapped old dude's girl or some shit. We need to handle this shit." Jacob said getting amped. This was the perfect opportunity to prove to people that he had what it took. He planned on taking over Atlanta and refused to let Nyah get all of the credit and reap the benefits. He'd take her out too, if he had to.

"That's all you got?" Nyah asked. She knew exactly who Jacob was talking about, but he had called her over here like he had some real information. Now that she had confirmation that her suspicions were true, she just needed to put a plan in motion.

Jacob watched her ass jiggle as she walked down the hall to her father's office. Jacob had always crushed on Nyah. She was a beautiful girl and when he imagined himself running things, he always envisioned her by his side. The only problem is Nyah saw herself as Queen and there could only be one leader in the castle. He needed a woman by his side that knew her place, not someone that would challenge his every move and decision. He knew Nyah was probably putting her own plan in motion, but he also had a plan. Nyah could fall in line or get taken care of with everybody else.

Chapter 18

Elijah had been calling Justice non-stop over the past week. He hadn't seen his son in a week and it was driving him crazy. He figured she would be over their loss by now. She needed to think about EJ and not be so selfish. He had finally grown tired of getting her voicemail, so he had driven over to her house.

The first thing he noticed was that her car was not parked in the driveway. Justice rarely used her garage, so he knew she hadn't pulled in there. Still, he got out of his car and used his key to enter the house. He had bought her the house and his son lived here, he didn't see anything wrong with him having a key.

He didn't hear any sounds anywhere in the house. He walked up the stairs to see if they were sleeping. Walking into her room, the first thing he noticed was her bed made neatly with clothes laid all over it. He didn't see her, so he walked down the hall to his son's room. His closet was open and he could see clothes missing. EJ's bed was also made. Elijah could see some of his toys were gone.

"Yo! Where the fuck you at with my son? Call me back ASAP. Don't make me come looking for you, Justice!" Elijah snapped on her voicemail as he walked back down the stairs and into the kitchen. Justice had him all the way fucked up.

Walking into the kitchen he noticed her cell phone on the counter with a note underneath it. He knew something was up.

Eli,

Since I was a little girl all I ever wanted to be was Mrs. Elijah Williams. First you broke my heart by leaving New York and me behind. Then the day I found out I was pregnant with EJ, I flew to Atlanta to surprise you. Only to find you with another woman in what you let me believe was our apartment. I can admit I was wrong for keeping EJ from you, but when you came back in our lives, I felt we could finally be a family. First you flaunt that Khloé girl in front of me, and then the ultimate disrespect was bringing that hoe up to the hospital the day I lost our baby. I realize I don't mean shit to you. You're selfish and I made it too easy for you by always bending backwards for whatever you wanted me to do. I just fit myself into whatever you had going on. You took me for granted. I allowed for everything that has happened between us. I refuse to stand for it anymore. It's time I get back to my life and live for Justice. Don't come for us, I'll call you when you can come get EJ. Please respect this time I need for myself.

Jus xx

"That's that bullshit!" Elijah shouted knocking everything off of the counter. He stormed out of the house slamming the door behind him. He sat in his car and hit the steering wheel a few times. How could Justice be so fucking selfish? She had already kept him from EJ for almost 2 years, and now she was taking him away again. She couldn't keep playing these games with his son. He called up Zane and told him to get on tracking her down quickly. After Zane said he was on it, Elijah pulled out of his driveway and off to the one person he needed the most right now.

******

BAM! BAM! BAM!

Khloé walked out of her bedroom towards the front door. Whoever was knocking on her door like the damn police better have had a good reason. Kai had finally started spending the night with Darren, so she was enjoying finally having her condo to herself. She had been online looking at new furniture. She felt it was time for a change with everything that had taken place over the last few months.

The knocking continued and nothing could prepare her for the sight on the other side. Elijah stood there with a devastated look across his sexy face. She had never seen him like this before. She wasn't sure what to do. Even though they hadn't spoken in a while, she couldn't turn him away. She didn't say anything, just opened the door wide enough to let him in. Elijah walked in and went straight to her bedroom.

"What's going on?" Khloé was trying to figure out why he was so upset.

Elijah didn't say anything. He lay on his back staring up at the ceiling. Everything Justice had written in her letter was true. He was selfish. She didn't see that she had broken his heart by leaving him, and he had never mentioned it to her. All the women he ran through meant nothing to him until Khloé. When Justice came back and with his son, he was very happy. He had a mini me that he loved more than anything in the world.

Elijah grew up without a father, or a mother really, and never wanted his kids to feel the way he had. Everything he had been doing to Justice the last few months was pushing her away. He just didn't think that when she finally got the hint that they would never be, she'd leave and take his son. He couldn't blame no one but himself.

"You want anything?" Khloé stood next to the bed unsure of what to do.

Elijah didn't answer. Instead, he pulled her down on top of him and held her close. He had messed things up with his childhood love, but refused to let things get that bad with Khloé. She was different from every other girl he'd come across in Atlanta. Some would say her innocence made her too naïve, and she'd never be able to handle a man like him, but that was exactly what he loved about her. She didn't fully know the life he lived. She wasn't after his money or fame, she just wanted him.

Khloé laid with her head on Elijah's chest. She missed these moments. They would lay up and watch a movie or just talk. She got to see a side of him no one else did. He always had to be someone else when they were out in public, but behind closed doors he was just Elijah.

"Justice left. She took my son." Elijah said finally breaking the silence.

Khloé's head shot up at his admission. Elijah could have treated Justice a lot better, but he was a good father to their son. She didn't understand what would make Justice just up and leave taking baby EJ away. She didn't know what to say so she just waited for him to continue.

"She lost our baby. She's blaming me for it. I loved that girl since we were 14 years old. I treated her like shit. I didn't even know I was doing it. She just wouldn't let go. I didn't want her like that no more." Elijah continued. "I didn't want to be all family with her one minute then out with the next bitch in front of her. I thought I was doing the right thing by being real with her. She had it in her head we were going to be a family."

Khloé listened as he spoke. She felt like he was just talking out loud and not really to her.

"Even though you hurt her, it's still not right for her to keep EJ from you. He's your son too and you already missed out on a lot of time with him. You should probably see about getting joint custody with her. Let her have her space for now, but you guys need to talk. It's not about you or her feelings, that baby needs both his parents."

Elijah fell silent thinking about everything Khloé just said. She was right, the only person who truly lost out in this situation was EJ. His son was caught in the middle of his parents' drama. Maybe filing for shared custody wouldn't be such a bad idea. He hoped Zane could find out something soon. He wanted to apologize to Justice and see his son. This was the longest he'd gone without seeing EJ since he brought him down from New York. He couldn't believe he let his stupid ways cost him time with his son.

Chapter 19

"So how far along are you now?" Eric asked looking at how huge Kai's belly had grown since the last time he saw her.

"Almost 9 months." Kai replied before spooning a huge pile of mashed potatoes into her mouth. She knew she shouldn't be here right now meeting with Eric, but if the baby was his, he did have a right to know what was going on.

"Is everything going okay? Do you need anything?" Eric asked before awkwardly reaching across the table and putting his hand on top of Kai's.

"Everything is fine. He is growing perfectly the doctor said." She snatched her hand back from him. She hoped she wasn't giving him the wrong idea by meeting up with him. She was doing this for her child, not to get back with him. Darren had her heart and there was nothing anyone could do about it.

"What about us? If the baby is mine, don't you think we should try and make this work?" Eric asked hopefully. There used to be a time when he had Kai wrapped around his fingers. He had Kennedy at home thinking their life was perfect. His family approved of her and their daughter. They were scheduled to be married in November. All Kai had to do was say the word, and he would call the wedding off with Kennedy. She was who he really loved.

"There is no us, Eric. You have Kennedy and I have Darren. This is just a messy situation. We all have to be adults about it." Kai was regretting agreeing to meet with him. By his actions, she could tell he still had hope for the two of them, but that was a road she would never go down again. He had strung her along for two years and made a lot of promises. Unfortunately, his time had run out and she had moved on to someone else.

Eric was more than fine. He was 6'2 full of muscle. His chocolate skin was smooth and even. He strongly resembled actor Morris Chestnut with his low cut hair and always well maintained goatee. He had the straightest set of white teeth. His smile alone could melt the panties off of any woman and he knew it. He came from a very well off family and had an excellent job as an entertainment lawyer. Even with all that going for him, he was just no match to Darren in her eyes.

"Come on now. You know I don't love her the way I love you."

"That doesn't matter anymore. I have moved on. I am no longer in love with you. I have someone I love very much." Kai said standing up. She was mad she didn't get to finish her meal. "I made a mistake coming here. I should go."

"Don't leave on my account." Darren said causing Kai to whip her head around too quickly, making her dizzy.

"Wha…What are you doing here?" Kai stuttered.

"I was meeting with Dutch like you wanted me to. Didn't even get a chance to talk to the nigga. I walk in and see you chopping it up with this nigga like shit is sweet. Here I am thinking I'm doing something good for the woman I love, and she can't even keep her promise." Darren said. Kai could see the anger burning like fire in his eyes.

"It's not what it looks like…" Kai began.

"You don't have to explain nothing to him." Eric cut her off. He didn't like the fact that she felt the need to explain herself to Darren. He didn't want to believe she had really moved on from. The love in her eyes was like a knife to his chest.

"The fuck you mean she don't have to explain herself." Darren shouted causing people to start to look their way. "This don't concern you, nigga. You got what you came for now leave. Until that baby is born, you don't have nothing to say to her. If you see her out, know that's me. You need to cross the street or lower your head. If I catch you near her again, won't be no words."

Eric was about to protest, but Darren lifted his shirt a little showing Eric his piece. He wasn't afraid to let it be known he was carrying. If Eric violated one more time he was more than willing to put some hot lead in his body. Luckily Eric got the message and walked out of the restaurant leaving Darren and Kai alone.

"Darren, baby, I—" Kai started to explain.

"Don't say shit else to me. It was your idea to not have any contact with the nigga. I get that he could be the father. I was going to meet you halfway. You sneaky as hell, ma, and I don't have no time for it. Call me when the baby is born." With that said, Darren turned and walked out of the restaurant. Kai wanted to go after him, but Dutch held her back.

"Let him go, baby girl. Arguing is only going to make it worse right now. Let him cool off and he'll come around." Dutch said rubbing her back to try and get her to calm down. He didn't want her to stress herself out and possibly cause harm to his grandchild. Kai only nodded her head with understanding. She and Darren clearly needed to have another talk.

******

"What the hell?" Kai cursed as she tried her key in the lock at Darren's house and it wouldn't turn. She couldn't see any lights on in the house or any cars in the driveway. It was a school night so where could he be? She attempted to dial his number once more, but he had already blocked her number. She dialed the only other person who might be able to help.

"Hello? Kai baby? Is everything okay?" Ms. Pam asked.

"Yeah. I was wondering if you knew where Darren was. I'm at the house and no one is here." Kai said hoping Ms. Pam didn't know what was going on between the two.

"I uh…"

Kai could hear her whispering to someone in the background. Figuring it was Darren that Ms. Pam was talking to, she hung up the phone. She got back in her car to drive over to Ms. Pam's house. Darren was trying to play games with her, and she didn't have time for it. He always ran or sent her away, but this time they were going to talk like adults. If that didn't work then she was done with him. She would just raise her baby all on her own without a father.

"What you come here for?" Darren asked with an attitude after he swung open the front door.

"We need to talk." Kai said and pushed her way into the house.

"Ain't shit to talk about. You don't know what the fuck you want. So I'm making it easy for you." Darren walked past her and sat on the couch before her.

"What are you saying?" Kai said breathlessly. His words cut her like a knife in the chest. She hoped he was speaking from a place of hurt and wasn't serious.

"I'm saying. You can't choose between me and that fuck boy, so I'm taking myself out the running. You the one said you didn't want to deal with ole boy, but you keep running back. I'ma let you have it." Darren said turning the TV on and flipping through channels like she wasn't even there.

Kai's eyes burned with tears. She wouldn't let him see her cry, though. She turned and without another word she left Ms. Pam's house. She was almost 9 months along and didn't have time to be forcing someone into something they clearly didn't want to. She would just talk to Khloé and Ace about her getting her own space for her and the baby. She had enough money saved up from modeling gigs and could afford to handle her own. She hoped Darren knew what he was doing. She wasn't going to keep doing this back and forth shit with him.

Chapter 20

The sky was gray and cloudy. The wind was blowing heavy as Nyah stood beside the final resting place for her father and brother. She was dressed to kill in a couture white pantsuit that she accented with gold accessories. She was the only one in attendance besides the pastor and funeral home director. Dame wasn't big on family and Jesse's mother seemed to not care that her only child had died. She had hung up the phone in Nyah's face when she called. The only person Nyah was missing was her mother. Her mother was never really there for her as a child, but Nyah figured she would at least show up for her on a day like this.

"Mommy!" A 9-year-old Nyah screamed as her mother came through the door.

"Yes, baby." Her mother said already sounding annoyed.

Nyah wanted to show her mother her new report card that held straight A's. She also had an award from her dance studio where she took modern and jazz dance. Nyah wanted to show her mother how good she was, and maybe her mother would take her with her this time. She hated how all the other girls in her dance class had mothers who would show up to every performance to do their hair and makeup while Nyah only had her nanny there.

"I got straight A's, Mommy! And outst…outstanding performance in my dance class!" She smiled really big and handing both things to her

mother. She watched as her mother read each paper and then handed them back to her. Nyah fought back tears as she watched her mother walk down the hall towards her father's study without so much as a good job.

Nyah sat on the couch quietly. She knew how much her mother hated when she cried. She looked through her bag again to make sure she had everything she needed. She had packed a bag in hopes that since she was being so good on this visit, her mother would take her home with her.

A few hours later, Nyah woke up. She had fallen asleep on the couch waiting for her mother to come out. She noticed it was dark outside. She ran down the hall and pushed her father's office door open only to find it empty. She ran back down the hall and looked out the front door. Her mother's shiny new car was no longer parked in the circular driveway. She ran upstairs to her room, slammed the door behind her, and cried into the pillow. She cried so hard she lost her voice and couldn't do anything but fall asleep.

"You want to say a few words?" The funeral director asked her, shaking her from her memories. She shook her head no as tears silently fell down her beautiful light brown skin. Her whole life her father had been the only one there for her. He told her that she was tough. She was a King and King's were strong. She remembered asking him at 12 years old why her last name was different from his, Jesse's, and her mother's.

"It doesn't matter what they call you. King blood flows through your veins and that's all that matters. Remember, King's are royalty." He'd said.

Nyah knew the day would come that she'd have to bury her father. There were only two ways out of the business he was in, dead or in jail. She had hoped he would be around to see her takeover his empire and make him proud. He would never get to see her married or have children. He was always on edge, and she would never get to see him carefree and retired. They had spent the last few years plotting to take over Atlanta. She found it funny how people always thought of these things after someone had passed. If she could go back, she would tell her father none of this was worth it just so she could have another moment with him.

Nyah looked up as she saw a car approaching. Out of the ghost white Bentley Continental GT convertible stood Olivia Jackson-Malone. Her blonde hair flowed flawlessly in the wind. She too was dressed in a vintage white Chanel pantsuit with no top on. Her 36C breasts sat perfectly like two ripened melons underneath the blazer. She wore a gold chain that hung right between her cleavage. She put on her black Chanel frames and began walking towards the burial site. People could call her mother all sorts of bitches and gold diggers, but Olivia was beyond beautiful.

Olivia didn't say a word. She half-hugged her daughter, who she hadn't seen in over a few years, then stood behind her to allow Nyah to continue to pay her respects. Olivia didn't feel anything towards the death of Dame. She never had any real feelings for him. The only reason she'd really dealt with him was off the strength of Nyah. She never wanted to have a baby by him, but he had begged her not to go through with the abortion.

"Please, I'm begging you, Livi. Don't kill my seed." Dame stood in the doctor's office pleading with Olivia. He had just found out through one of the medical assistants he was sleeping with that she was scheduled for an abortion. He knew Olivia didn't have feelings for him, she was just using him to fill the void from Ace being gone.

"I can't. I'll lose my husband and mdy girls." Olivia said.

"I'll take the baby. You won't have to tell Ace anything. I'll raise her on my own." Dame begged again.

That's exactly what he'd done. Olivia knew she should feel ashamed for giving her daughter away, but she didn't. Even after Ace had divorced her and abandoned their family, she always held on in hopes that he would come back to her. There was no way she'd be able to explain another child, especially one not by him. Nyah looked just like Olivia, but she had light brown skin. Underneath her weave were natural silky curls like Chilli from TLC. There would have been no way she could have denied her.

Olivia admired the setup of the funeral. Both Dame and Jesse were being laid to rest in white coffins with 18k gold plated accents. They had black tombstones with pictures of their faces engraved into the stone. "HERE LIES A KING" was the caption beneath their birth and death information. There was a case off to the side that Olivia was sure held doves to be released. She waited patiently for Nyah to finish paying her respects, but it was getting cold outside. She was about to say something when a car pulled up.

A huge black Escalade pulled behind Olivia's Bentley. Out stepped Elijah looking like he'd just stepped off the pages of GQ magazine in a casual Tom Ford look from head to toe. He had flowers in his hand. Nyah began to panic. She had told him she was burying her father today, but she never planned for him to come. She told him it was something she wanted to do alone. He said he understood, but clearly he hadn't respected her wishes. As he approached, Nyah reached in her bag and put her hand on her gun. She walked towards him to meet him halfway.

Olivia noticed the tension in Nyah as the young man approached. She took off her shades to get a better look at him. He was fine as hell. The way his black sweater hugged his arms showed off his muscular build. Her daughter had good taste.

"You didn't have to come." Nyah said meeting him halfway between the cars and the burial. She didn't want him to get a look at the tombstones and reveal her identity. She didn't want him to know just yet. She was still trying to figure out a way to use their relationship to her advantage.

"I heard you, ma. But when you said you had no family to call, I just wanted to be here if you need me." Elijah could sense the awkwardness in her body language. He wasn't sure what she was thinking. He thought she'd be excited that he came. He handed her the flowers. She stood there holding them waiting for him to leave.

"Nyah, honey, who's your friend?" Olivia said walking up. She had watched their exchange from afar and could see how uncomfortable her daughter was. She decided to walk over and see if she could help out.

Elijah looked confusedly between Nyah and who he assumed was her mother. He recognized Olivia from somewhere, but couldn't figure out from where. The way her blue eyes sparkled made him feel uncomfortable. She was too familiar.

"Nyah? I thought your name was Bria. Who the fuck is a Nyah?" Elijah said angrily.

Nyah looked at her mother wishing she'd never come. She then looked to the ground trying to come up with a reason why she lied about her name. Olivia offered no assistance and turned to walk back towards the graves. She figured it was time to put Dame and Jesse in the ground so everyone could leave. Whatever Nyah had going on was about to get really messy.

"Um… I don't know what to say." Nyah said shifting from foot to foot. She was getting extremely nervous under Elijah's intense stare. She could see him clench his jaw in frustration.

"Who the fuck are you?" Elijah asked her. He couldn't believe he'd allowed this woman into his life, and he didn't even know who the fuck she was.

Just as Nyah was going to answer, they heard shouting. Nyah took this opportunity to run over to where her mother was in a heated argument with the funeral director.

"Ma'am, Miss Jackson requested the dove release as the bodies were lowered. We can't do it until she tells us!" The old man shouted at Olivia. She was trying to rush him to just lower the bodies, but there was a process for everything.

"My daughter is ready to go NOW! Put the damn bodies in the ground so we can go!" Olivia shouted back.

"Mom, it's okay." Nyah said then turned to the director. "We're going to leave now. You can release the doves and lower the bodies."

"Nyah Jackson…" Elijah was trying to figure out where he'd heard her name before. Something weird was going on. He had a million questions racing through his mind, but decided to be respectful of the situation. She was there to bury her father and brother. They would be talking right after. He stood behind her next to her mother as the pastor read Psalm 23.

"*The Lord is my shepherd; I shall not want. He maketh me to lie down in green pastures: he leadeth me beside the still waters. He restoreth my soul: he leadeth me in the paths of righteousness for his name's sake. Yea, though I walk through the valley of the shadow of death, I will fear no evil: for thou art with me; thy rod and thy staff they comfort me. Thou prepares a table before me in the presence of mine enemies: thou anointest my head with oil; my cup runneth over. Surely goodness and mercy shall follow me all the days of my life: and I will dwell in the house of the Lord forever.*"

Elijah watched on as the funeral director then released the doves and the cemetery staff began lowering the caskets in the ground. Whoever Nyah was, he could tell she really loved her father. Even though she had deceived him, he still placed his hand on her back as she cried.

"That concludes the service today." The funeral director said dismissing everyone. He threw a hateful glance at Olivia before he walked away towards his waiting car. He pulled his phone out of his pocket to text Zane to look into Nyah Jackson, but it slipped from his hands. He bent down to pick it up. It wasn't until that moment Elijah noticed the names on the headstones; Damien "Dame" King and Jesse Damien King. Nyah Jackson… *Jesse's sister*! He reached in his waistband to pull his gun but heard one cock next to him. He held his hands up in surrender, but he was looking for a way to get out the situation.

"I don't know what you think you know, but here's what the fuck is going to happen. You are going to get in your car and drive away. There will be no shoot out at my father's funeral." Nyah said seriously. Any other day, she'd happily bust guns with Elijah and kill him, but today was about her father and she would not disrespect him in that manner. If she knew Elijah had pulled the trigger on Dame, she would probably feel differently. She would have emptied her full clip into his head and left him there to rot.

The pastor watched on in horror. Olivia was trying to find a way to sneak past the altercation and get back to her car. The pastor started praying and knelt behind another headstone as Olivia got on all fours in her pantsuit and began crawling towards the street where her car was parked. She didn't care about grass stains or dirt on her all white suit. She just wanted to live. She was about 20 feet away from her car when she stood to run.

POP! POP! POP!

Shots rang out as Mitch stepped out of the Escalade and began firing shots towards Nyah. Elijah ducked off behind a statue and pulled his gun. There was smoke everywhere as shots rang out from every direction. Suddenly all the gun fire ceased. He stood to assess the scene when he noticed a Bentley starting up.

Tires screeched as Olivia and Nyah pulled off in Olivia's Bentley. Mitch then turned and began firing shots at the back of the car shattering her rear window. Olivia and Nyah both screamed as the glass flew at the back of their heads. Nyah turned and aimed her gun out the busted window and began returning shots at Mitch who ran for cover. He opened the door to the SUV and used it as a shield since it was bulletproof. He kept firing until Nyah and Olivia were out of sight.

Sirens could be heard in the distance. Elijah pulled all the cash out of his pocket, about $5,400, and gave it to the pastor before running and hopping in the truck. He and Mitch then sped out of the cemetery. He pulled out his phone to call Darren and Zane and tell them what was up.

"Yo!" He yelled as soon as Darren was on the phone. "You would never believe who this bitch Bria really is!"

"Who the fuck is a Bria?" Darren asked. He sounded like he just woke up.

"That little west side hoe I been smashing. I went to check on her today at her pops' funeral. I find out that *Bria* is not this bitch's real name!" Elijah was heated. He needed to slow down. Pussy was not worth all the trouble. She now knew where he laid his head as well as the location of several of his businesses. He had simply not given a fuck when he was parading her around town the last couple of months. She had even been inside his townhouse. She could have been in his home going through all sorts of shit.

"Oh…" Darren said remembering who Elijah was talking about.

"That bitch is Nyah Jackson… That pussy ass Jesse's sister. She was burying those mufuckas today." Elijah then went on to explain everything that had transpired at the funeral, leaving Darren speechless.

"Damn!" Darren finally said after a few minutes. He told Elijah to hold on as he got another phone call.

Elijah hung up. He knew Darren would call him back. He began calling around putting 50 grand out on any information on Nyah. He needed to get to her and fast. No telling what all she had seen or overheard while she was around him. He had not been thinking clearly. His mind was all fucked up over Khloé and Justice's pregnancy. He ran his hand over his hair in frustration then took the blunt from Mitch and took a long pull.

Chapter 21

"What the fuck you mean it was all seized!" Elijah shouted at Black. Today was supposed to be one of his largest shipments coming in by cargo plane. Black had just explained to him that when he pulled up to the airstrip, there were a dozen or more unmarked SUVS unloading the plane and arresting the pilot.

Elijah wasn't worried about the pilot being arrested. There was half a million dollars' worth of product on that plane and it had all been taken. He couldn't believe that. His shipments were always air tight, he never had a problem. He prayed to God that no one on his team was snitching, because he would hate to have to kill that mother fucker and their whole family.

Black stood nervously off to the side as Elijah went around kicking and breaking things around the house. It wasn't his house so he wasn't going to stop him. Hell, the stolen product was effecting his pockets as well. If he wasn't sure Elijah would haul off and shoot him if he moved too fast, Black would join him in breaking shit.

After about five minutes, Elijah calmed down enough. Not wanting to look around at all the scared faces in the room, he stepped outside and lit a blunt before calling up Darren to give him the run down.

"You never gon' believe this shit." Elijah said as soon as Darren picked up.

"I just heard. Never had no problems out of Miami, and now shit getting busted left and right." Darren said too calmly letting Elijah know he was more than angry.

"Miami! What the fuck, yo! I'm talking about the drop supposed to be out in Augusta. Meet me at the spot, yo. We need to get to the bottom of this shit." Elijah shouted then hung up the phone without waiting on a response from Darren. He then took the burner phone, took out the battery and put them both in a random cup of liquor he saw on the porch. He had a couple of them and always made sure to switch them up regularly.

For years he and Darren had been moving their product the same way. Only occasionally switching up days and modes of transportation. Because they had a number of government officials on their payroll, they had never had any problems. Now two drops had been raided and no one knew anything. That shit just wasn't adding up.

He texted Ace from his personal line and told him to meet up with he and Darren. Ace was probably the only person he could trust to get to the bottom of this shit here. Usually they would get a warning when someone was sniffing around their operation, but his phone had been silent. Silence meant that business was running as usual. Now someone or some people were trying to fuck that up for them.

He went and hopped in his S65 AMG Benz and set out for the spot. He and Darren had recently purchased an industrial park off of Peachtree Industrial Blvd. They owned several trucks and were thinking about expanding that business a little more. They had their hands in several business and trucking was one of their most successful ventures. It also provided them a way to transport large quantities of their product. Pulling up to the spot, he could already see both their cars out front letting him know they were inside.

"What's up?" Elijah greeted both Darren and Ace by dapping them up.

"This shit is crazy." Darren said. The whole situation Ace was filling him in on before Elijah walked in. Both of them were in the area so they arrived quickly.

"What you know." Elijah said firing up another blunt. His nerves were real bad. He felt like killing everything moving, but he knew better. By the looks on Darren and Ace's faces he knew it was about to get worse.

"Somebody got it out bad for you niggas. Your names not popping up on everybody's desk just yet, but after today, I'm sure you will. Whoever we dealing with got major connections. They were able to bypass a lot of paperwork and go directly to the top. This shit is serious. Since there's no paper trail, it's going to be hard to erase it." Ace gave them the run down.

Darren ran his hands down his face. He was trying real hard to go the legit route. Other than that little dude he popped back in East Point and Sean, his hands have been clean. He has been spending all his time with his family and at the label. He purposefully left this shit to Elijah so none of this would be happening. Now it was looking like he'd have to step back into the bullshit.

"So we got a snitch or some shit?" Elijah wasn't sure how to process the information. He could throw money at the situation and make his name disappear from a database, but there was no paper trail. With all the drugs that were seized today, he'd be looking at a couple of life sentences, he didn't have time for that bullshit. If there was a snitch, he could intimidate them and hope they took the bait or just get rid of them completely. From what it sounds like, someone on the inside is keeping everything air tight. He knew Ace wasn't working with the bureau like that anymore, but he had guys on the inside who'd do anything for him.

"I don't know, young buck. We have to wait until shit gets processed today and see what it's looking like tomorrow. Keep your eyes low and your nose clean. They going to be watching you." Ace warned. He hoped that Elijah was listening. The amount of drugs the FBI had attached to him and Darren wasn't a good look at all. Ace smelled a set-up, though, and he'd definitely be getting to the bottom of it.

"What about the connect?" Elijah said to Darren. They no longer got their shit on consignment, but paid up front for it every re-up, so money wasn't an issue. The issue would be if the connect no longer wanted to work with them because their names and spots were hot.

"Don't worry about that. He cool." Darren shrugged his shoulders.

"How the fuck he going to be cool. We just lost over a million dollars in drugs. The fucking Feds is watching! He ain't gon' give us shit." Elijah said. He could no longer hold in his anger. They had just lost everything and the possibility of their connect not allowing them to replace the product was too much for him to handle. He had more than enough money saved up to walk away. It was just the principle of the matter.

"Because I'm gon' be cool, lil nigga." Dutch said walking into the warehouse and joining the men where they stood.

"Shut the fuck up." Elijah said giving Dutch some dap. He didn't believe what Dutch was implying right now.

Darren clenched his jaw at the sight of Dutch. He wasn't sure how to deal with his father/mentor. Over the years he'd looked to Dutch as a father figure with no problems, but finding out that he was his actual father was a tough pill to swallow. They had met up to talk about it, but that ended up going left when he saw Kai eating lunch with Eric.

Ace and Elijah noticed the tension between Dutch and Darren. Usually the two would be joking back and forth, but they both stood awkwardly across from each other not saying a word. Ace had an idea of what the tension was about, but Elijah was lost.

"The fuck wrong with y'all?" He asked breaking the silence.

"Ask this nigga." Darren said through clenched teeth. Every time he looked at Dutch, he realized how much they actually resembled one another. It was infuriating to him.

"Now is not the time." Dutch said. He had been trying to reach out to his son, but Darren had yet to respond.

"Well somebody better tell me something!" Elijah said. Part of it was him being nosy, but the other reason was he'd always admired the two's relationship. He and Darren both grew up without fathers, so the fact that Darren got to have that type of bond in Dutch was amazing to him.

"I ain't got shit to say!" Darren shouted before walking away leaving Elijah real confused.

"Don't walk away from me, *son*!" Dutch shouted after him causing Darren to freeze in his tracks. This was the first time Dutch had actually referred to him as family.

"I need a chair and some popcorn for this shit." Elijah said handing the blunt to Ace who agreed. "First, this nigga is the plug after all these years. And now you niggas trying to say he's your daddy? Damn."

Darren had nothing further to say. If they weren't discussing business, he didn't want to talk about shit. He had told Dutch many times over the years how he felt like if he had parents growing up his life would have been much different. Dutch had just listened to him pour out his feelings and not said a word. Darren didn't understand how he could just do that. Darren felt such a sense of pride when it came to DJ. He wanted to be a part of every aspect of his son's life.

Chapter 22

Kai called Darren for the third time since she woke up this morning. It was the day of her 36 week appointment to check on the baby. It was getting closer to her due date, and she was almost full term. She wanted to make sure Darren was ready for the arrival of what she hoped was their new baby. They hadn't spoken at all since the incident with Eric, and her coming to Ms. Pam's house. She wanted to make things right before the baby came. She didn't want to bring her child into the world with all the chaos going on.

Kai was growing impatient waiting for him to come around. She could no longer drive herself around and had hoped Darren would be there to drive her. She had given him enough time to cool off. She was tired of the back and forth with him. If he didn't want to be with her, it would hurt like hell, but she'd learn to live with it. Her baby wasn't even here yet, and she felt he was already neglecting his fatherly duties. Even if they weren't cool, he could still pick up the phone on the strength of the baby. She could be in labor or anything right now.

There was only an hour before her appointment and still no word from Darren. She called him one last time, but still didn't get an answer. She knew Khloé was out with Malik, or Elijah, so she didn't want to bother her. She had gotten more comfortable with her father being around, but she didn't feel comfortable enough to allow him to accompany her to the appointment. She was getting ready to request for an Uber when her phone began to ring. She didn't recognize the number but she answered anyways.

"Hello?" Kai answered hesitantly.

"Don't hang up." Eric said hopefully. "I was wondering if you would let me come to the appointment today, I want to be there."

Kai thought about it. If he was at work then he could definitely pick her up and make it to the appointment on time. If Darren wanted to act like a child then that was his problem.

"Okay. Pick me up or we're going to be late." Kai considered if she was making the right decision as the words came out of her mouth. Something was telling her not to go through with it, but it was too late. Eric was already saying goodbye and hanging up. She could hear the excitement in his voice. Against her better judgement, Kai went to grab her purse so she could meet him downstairs in the lobby.

******

"Well, Ms. Malone, everything looks great. Baby is doing very well. You should pack your bag for the hospital, he could come any day now." The doctor said while handing Kai a wipe to get the gel off of her belly. "Do any of you have any questions?"

Darren stood to leave, he had no questions. He really had no words for anybody. He was irritated at the fact that she had brought that little fuck boy up there with her. It took everything in him not to make a scene when they walked in together. Kai was definitely showing him her true colors.

Wanting to get out of the room and away from the obvious tension, Kai said no at the same time Eric said yes. Eric wanted to know if it were possible to get a DNA test done before the baby came. He was ready to get rid of Darren out of their lives once and for all. In his mind, he would leave Kennedy for Kai and they'd be one big happy family. His question caused Darren to stop at the door. He wanted to know the answer as well. All this bullshit could be over with.

"It is possible, but I don't recommend it. Kai is too far along in her pregnancy, and I don't want to risk any complications. When she has the baby we can have the results rushed and back from the lab within 24 hours." The doctor informed them.

Once the doctor finished speaking, Darren continued out of the door. He could feel her watching her the entire time the doctor spoke, but he had nothing to say to Kai. The fact that she ran back to Eric and had him coming to her appointments spoke volumes. She didn't know what she wanted and Darren wasn't about to play no games with her.

Kai's heart dropped to her stomach seeing him go. When she wanted him to come pick her up earlier, she had hoped they would get a chance to talk. She realized the mistake she had made in bringing Eric. She should have just come alone. Still, Darren was still overreacting to the situation. Everything he was doing, was pushing her right back into the arms of Eric. If he wanted her, he should be putting up more of a fight. She was confused and not sure what to do. She knew who she wanted, but he wasn't acting like he felt the same way.

"You ready, babe?" Eric asked Kai. He wanted to take her to lunch and then go shopping for baby items. He wasn't sure if she needed anything for the baby. She had ignored him for most of her pregnancy, and now that she was opening up, he wanted to make sure she understood he was there for her. He had a whole nursery built for his son at his parents' house. Kennedy didn't want anything to do with his son, and that was okay with him.

"Don't call me babe." Kai said with an attitude. She walked out of the room and went and sat in the waiting room. Pulling out her phone she called up Khloé to come pick her up. This whole situation was getting messier by the minute and she needed some advice. She needed to talk to her twin and get an outside opinion on what was going wrong between her and Darren.

"What are you doing? You want to grab lunch?" Eric sat down next to her. He was confused on her sudden change in attitude. He knew pregnant women often had mood swings, so he wasn't sure what he'd done to set her off. He wanted to keep by her side until the baby was born and maybe she'd let him come up to the hospital.

"I'm waiting on Khloé. It was a mistake to have you here today. I'm sorry." Kai sniffled trying to fight her tears. "When I go into labor, I don't want you there. I will do the test first with Darren, and if the baby is not his, then I will call you up there. Don't call me. Just leave." Kai was on the verge of tears. Every little thing set her off these days, and there was nothing she could do to control it.

"Why do you keep acting like you know the baby's not mine?" Eric asked, his voice laced with anger. It seemed as though Kai had just cut him out of the situation. Why even bother to tell him there was a possibility he was the father, when she had already chosen? Pissed, but not wanting to cause a scene, Eric stood and left without a word.

******

"You did what?" Khloé asked in disbelief. Kai couldn't be serious with all the poor choices she had been making lately.

"I just figured since Darren was acting like he didn't want to be there then at least one of my baby daddies could be present." Kai shrugged. She looked between her twin and Jazzy seeing that both their faces showed that they disapproved of her decision.

"Darren is only reacting to you. First you sneak and see Eric behind his back and he has to deal with that. Then you say you won't contact Eric until the baby is born. only to get caught having lunch with him. Now you're inviting him to your doctor's appointments. He doesn't know how to take the situation. You and Eric have a history. Darren is probably feeling like you're going to choose Eric over him in the end. You sure you know what you want?" Jazzy tried to explain Darren's side of things. She didn't want to hurt Kai's feelings, but she needed her to see that her decisions weren't just affecting her, but her relationship as a whole. Darren was a good man and Kai wasn't doing anything but pushing him away.

Kai took in everything Jazzy just said. She had been going about everything wrong. She was trying to make sure that whomever the father turned out to be, didn't feel slighted on time with their unborn, but she should have been more focused on making her relationship work. She felt bad for not seeing things from Darren's perspective. She was going to do everything in her power to make things right.

Chapter 23

Olivia stepped out of her car at the valet of the Ritz Carlton Atlanta. A chill ran up her spine as she handed her keys to the valet. She had been feeling like someone was following her for the last few days. She hurriedly walked around her rental and into the safety of the hotel lobby. Crossing the floor, she went to the elevator and rode up to the 10th floor. Approaching her door, she got a funny feeling in the pit of her stomach like something was wrong. Once again she shook off the bad vibes and entered her room.

Walking into the living room area of her suite, she kicked off her shoes and began to undress before a light flicked on in the corner of the room. There sat her baby's father, Ace, with a gun on his lap. When she looked into his brown eyes, her tanned skin turned a ghostly white as fear ran through her body. Even though she was scared by his presence, she had to admit Ace looked sexy as hell sitting there. She knew he was there to kill her, but her sex had a mind of its own as it soaked through her panties. Her first mind told her to turn and run, but fear of getting shot in the back had her stuck where she stood

"Sit over there." He pointed at the chair with his gun. She wasn't sure how to take this meeting. She was too scared to say anything, so she just stared at him as she sat in the chair across from him and watched as he lit up a cigarette. He placed the gun on the table in front of them, but she knew he had another somewhere else. She wouldn't risk going for it and wind up getting shot anyways.

"What do you want?" Olivia's voice was barely a whisper.

Ace ignored her question. He wasn't really sure what he was going to do with Olivia. Hurting her would also hurt his girls. Though they didn't have a relationship with her, Olivia was still their mother. There was a chance that they could want her around later on, especially now that Kai is about to have a baby. He sat and puffed on his cigarette as he thought back to when he first met Olivia Jackson.

Twenty five years ago…

"Who brought the white girl?" Dame asked pointing to Olivia. Everyone looked to where he was pointing.

"I don't know, but she could get it." Sean joked.

Olivia was easily the prettiest girl in the room. Not because she was white, but because she had this energy about her. Her blue eyes were warm and inviting and she smiled a lot. Ace had been watching her the whole night as she turned down man after man. She bought her own drinks and danced with her friends. He wanted to go speak to her, but he was kind of shy.

Olivia was at her three drink limit. She could feel eyes on her as she sipped her drink and swayed to the music. She didn't know why she let her friend, Angie, talk her into coming to this bar. She was the only white person in the building and stuck out like crazy. Guys kept approaching her, but she wasn't interested. She only wanted to come out and have a good time. Plus, she was a virgin. She knew they were only interested in sex. She felts a pair of eyes on her the whole night, but she could never find them in the crowd.

"What the fuck is he doing here?" Angela yelled. Her baby-daddy, Sean, was supposed to be at home with their son, not in the bar with random bitches in his lap. "I'm going over there."

"I know that's right." Another girl that was out with them, Monique, said.

All three girls approached the table where the guys were.

"What the fuck, Sean? This how we doing it now?" Angie shouted at him. Sean's eyes popped out his head when he heard her voice. He pushed the girl from his lap, grabbed Angie's arm, and pulled her towards the door. He had some explaining to do.

"Y'all want to chill with us til your girl comes back?" Dame asked. He was eyeing Monique like she was a juicy steak.

"Sure." Monique said and being forward, she sat on his lap.

Olivia took the seat next to Ace. She looked into his brown eyes and got lost for a moment. They appeared to be staring right back into her soul.

"Dominic." He said introducing himself. Shocked that he'd used his government name.

"Olivia." She said simply.

The rest was history. They had talked the whole night and were inseparable ever since then. Her family hated the fact that she was dating a black man, so they disowned her. Ace paid for her to finish school, but she ended up dropping out. She was pregnant with the twins, and they were married within the year. Those were the good old days.

Ace watched Olivia as she squirmed in her seat. He let her sit there for a minute before he got up and picked up an envelope he had sat on the table. He shook his head as he thumbed through the pages seeing all her lies and deception in front of him. Olivia wasn't sure what was in the envelope, but she could tell it angered him. Murder danced in his eyes, something she'd never seen from him before.

"Go ahead and take a look." Ace said too calmly as he handed her all the envelopes contents.

Pictures of her and Dame from 20 years ago, Nyah's birth certificate, a letter from their supposed divorce lawyer, and *an abortion receipt.* Olivia flipped through everything twice. There was no way she was going to get out of this alive.

"How did you find all this?" Olivia asked.

"Come on, O, you know me." Ace said. He had been sitting on this information for a while now. He just never acted on it because everyone had stayed in their lane. Since Kai's kidnapping he had been wondering what to do with all of it. The decision to off Dame was an easy one. That nigga deserved everything he got and more. He just didn't know what to do about Olivia.

At one point he would have given his own skin to save her, but she had done some unbelievable things over the years. She had fucked over a lot of people. He wasn't the only one wanting a piece of her. Olivia thought she was so smart, but he had been paying off people left and right to not come for her. As her husband, it was his duty. He can't believe she never filed the divorce papers. Just the thought had his blood boiling all over. He needed something besides this weak ass cigarette. He got up and walked over to the bar.

"What are you going to do?" Olivia asked quietly.

"So you fucked Dame, huh?" Ace said as he downed a shot of Jack before pouring another.

Olivia didn't know what to say, so she just sat and waited for him to say more.

"Then you actually had a baby for that nigga?" Ace shook his head in disbelief. He wasn't really talking to her at this point. Just finally saying everything out loud.

"Dominic, I—" Olivia started to say but was cut off.

"You aborted *my* child, though?" He shook his head. This shit was too much. "What? You wanted that nigga? You could have said that shit. I would have let you have it."

"I didn't know whose baby it was! He begged me to keep Nyah! I didn't want him. I wanted you. Why you think I went through all of this?" She cried.

Ace wasn't moved by her tears. He couldn't even believe what she was saying. She was possibly pregnant for another man twice, but she wanted him? What kind of shit was she on? She played the fuck out of him. The worst part was he was still in love with her. Not once in 12 years did he consider moving on. Yeah, he fucked around with a bunch of randoms, but nothing serious. Olivia had "remarried" 4 times and slept with his ex-friend.

Olivia got up and walked up to him. She could see the pain in his expression. This whole time she'd been acting foolishly by trying to hurt him, but seeing him hurt was too much for her. She wished she could go back and undo all her wrongs, but it was too late now.

"When you left me, I slipped up. He was there and one thing led to another. I found out I was pregnant. I had sex with you and him within 2 days. I couldn't keep the baby. So I took care of him…it." Realizing what she said she moved quickly to the other side of the room.

"A BOY! You fucking killed my son!" Ace threw the glass at her head. He had to get out of this room before he killed her. He hadn't decided what he really wanted to do, so it's best if he left now before he made a decision he'd later regret. He had his girls to think about and that was the only reason she was still breathing right now.

"Don't! We can talk about it. We don't know if he was yours." Olivia begged. She didn't want him to go. She would be looking over her shoulder every few minutes trying to see if he was coming for her. She needed to know where they stood today.

"Ain't shit to talk about." Ace then went over to the chair he sat in when she came in and picked up a bag. He pulled out a folder and handed it to her. "Sign this shit so I can go."

Olivia's eyes popped out of her head as she looked down at the divorce papers. Ace was not asking for much. He wanted her to change her name, and he'd also be giving her 5 million dollars. Olivia tried not to look too happy at the sight of the number. "You want a divorce?"

"I wanted one 11 years ago! Don't act surprised! Sign the shit so I can go!" He shoved a pen in her hand.

Olivia didn't move. She had no choice but to sign it, but if she figured out a way to get out of this she would. None of her other marriages were legal. She feared that if he actually filed these papers then Gregg might find out they weren't actually married. Why couldn't he just walk away and no one would have to know.

"Hurry the fuck up!" Ace cocked his gun and placed it to the side of her face. At one point he loved her more than anything, but right now he only saw the bitch who killed his son. She knew how much he wanted one and they had tried and tried, but she never got pregnant. He wondered how many more of his seeds she'd killed.

Olivia quickly signed all the places on the paperwork. Tears fell down her cheeks and onto the pages. She couldn't believe it had ended this way. The only man she'd ever loved had a gun to her face and forced her into a divorce. She handed him the papers back before falling to the floor crying.

Ace tucked his gun back and lifted her off of the ground by her throat.

"You're dead to me. Don't contact me or my kids. If I even hear your name around them, I'll fucking kill you."

He threw her on the ground and walked out of the room. Olivia laid on the floor gasping for air. Her tears were now mixed with snot as she cried it out. She knew he would make good on his promise. It was time for her to return to Gregg once and for all.

Chapter 24

"This tour going to be wild, yo." Elijah said looking over the itinerary for the spring tour Darren was putting together for some of their artists. They were hitting every major city on every coast. They had special feature artists coming through as well. He was counting up the ticket sales in his head already.

"Yeah. The team been working real hard on it." Darren stated proudly. This label was like his child. The whole time he was in prison he had been praying Elijah hadn't run it to the ground. When he got out it was doing well, but in the almost year since he'd been out, their revenue had tripled.

"That's what's up." Elijah said. He was glad Darren was sticking to keeping up with staying out of trouble. Those three years without his brother by his side were rough. Elijah wasn't a sit behind the desk, boardroom man. He preferred to be in the streets and clubs. Well the old him did. Now all he could think about while watching Darren was settling down with Khloé and making shit official.

"So you thinking about doing a song and coming on tour or you staying in retirement?" Darren asked.

"Nah. I don't think—" Elijah was cut off as the office door came crashing down.

"What the fuck?" Darren shouted as about 10 cops came rushing through the door and wrestled Elijah to the ground.

"Elijah Williams?" One of the cops asked after he was already in cuffs and being lifted off the ground.

Elijah simply nodded. He knew not to agitate the situation any further. Darren would call up their lawyer, and he'd be out in a few hours. He would be cooperative until then.

"You're under arrest for drug trafficking and continuing a criminal enterprise..." The cop began reading him his rights as they walked him out of the office.

The entire staff watched on as Elijah was escorted out of the office and out of the building. When the front doors open there were about two dozen paparazzi out front snapping pictures. Elijah then figured he was set up by someone.

About four hours later, Elijah was still sitting in an interrogation room. No one had come to speak with him or tell him anything. He knew something was wrong with the whole situation. He hadn't been allowed to make a phone call or use the bathroom. He knew Darren was on the outside working to get him out, so he didn't trip about speaking with his lawyer. He knew not to say anything until she was present.

******

"Recording artist and record executive Elijah Williams who goes by the stage name Ghost, was arrested this afternoon at his office. According to TMZ, he was charged with drug trafficking and continuing a criminal enterprise amongst other charges. More on this story later."

Khloé stared at the TV in disbelief. She knew what Elijah did for a living, but to see his face all over the news like that was still shocking. She was scrolling through Facebook on her phone when she saw the report pop up on several different blogs. After sitting for a moment she got up and started throwing on clothes. She dialed Darren's number and put it on speaker as she got ready. She was going to go down there and see what she could do. Those were serious charges he was facing.

"*You have reached the voicemail of Darren Price—*"

Khloé hung up the phone. He was probably on the phone with a lawyer or somebody. It said that Elijah was arrested from their office so that's where she was heading. She opted to hop in her Lexus truck and drive down there instead of the Bentley. She drove as fast as she could on the 45 minute drive. She hated Atlanta traffic, you couldn't get anywhere and these people can't drive for nothing.

An hour and 20 minutes later she was attempting to pull up in front of the building, but it was blocked off by police cruisers. She could see cops going in and out carrying boxes. She wasn't sure what was going on. She doubted Darren could talk right now, so she called the next person she could think of.

"Hey, baby girl." Ace answered still sounding asleep.

"Daddy!" Khloé cried. "The arrested Elijah! I don't know what to do! They're raiding his offices and everything."

Ace immediately woke up hearing the pain in his daughter's voice.

"Shhh. It's okay, baby girl. I'm going to make a few calls and see what all I can find out. Go back home and wait for me to call. I'll let you know when I find something out." Ace tried to speak calmly as to not alarm her. He knew what Elijah and Darren were into. Most likely it wasn't Atlanta PD who had arrested Elijah, it was the Feds. The Feds didn't come for you unless they were sure they had a case. Ace wasn't sure what he could do, but he still had some connections on the inside, who could let him know what was going on.

"Okay, Daddy." Khloé was sniffling into the other side of the phone.

"You have to be strong right now. Elijah can't be worried about you while he's in there. You want to be with a man like that, then you have to be prepared for what it come with." Ace warned her. He wouldn't have chosen a man in this lifestyle for his daughters, but he couldn't choose who they loved either.

"Kay." Khloé said and began wiping the tears from her eyes.

"Okay. I'll call you in a few." Ace said hanging up. He began making calls to see what all Elijah was being charged with and held on.

******

Elijah was still sitting on the same hard chair in the interrogation room when the door finally opened. A tall white man entered the room. He looked to be in his thirties. He had red hair, hazel eyes, and freckles all over his face. He didn't speak at first. He started spreading papers and photos all over the table in front of Elijah. Elijah didn't move to touch anything. He had a high priced lawyer on his payroll, and it was her job to read the paperwork and figure this shit out.

"I'm Agent Johnson. So you already know why you're here." The agent began. Elijah wished he could wipe the smirk off of his crooked as face.

"Actually, I have no idea. I wish you would hurry up and let me know, so I can call my lawyer and get the fuck out of here." Elijah said with a smirk of his own causing the agent to laugh.

"Mr. Williams or is it *Ghost*? You are facing some serious charges. You may want to take this seriously." Agent Johnson warned him, but Elijah didn't care. He knew none of these bullshit ass charges wouldn't hold. His business was airtight. The only way the Feds could be after him was if somebody snitched. He hoped that wasn't the case, but he didn't mind taking whoever it was out.

"You can call me Mr. Williams." Elijah said. "Now are you going to allow me to call my lawyer, or are you going to continue to hold me here and violate my rights?"

"Are your rights being violated?" Agent Johnson asked sarcastically. "I don't remember you asking for your lawyer."

"I am asking now. Make that happen for me. Thanks, Tim." Elijah said reading the ID badge off the agent's coat.

Agent Johnson's face flushed hot with anger. Elijah was speaking to him like he was the help and he was being inconvenienced. He had never dealt with anyone so rude before. They usually came in singing trying to roll over on their so-called friends so they could go home. Elijah's confidence had the seasoned agent shook.

"Can you bring me some water or coffee or something?" Elijah added as the agent stood to leave. He knew he was only adding fuel to the fire, but he didn't care. These punk ass cops had no idea who they were dealing with.

Agent Johnson opened the door and a gorgeous black woman entered the room.

"Mr. Williams, hold tight. They're processing your release, and then I'll have you out of here." Elijah's lawyer spoke.

Tierrany Mayfield was one of the top criminal attorneys in the city. She had a $20,000 retainer and only took on high profile cases. She was somewhat of a bitch in person, but she felt that was the only way to get respect in this male dominated industry. She had a 90% success rate in winning cases. Elijah and Darren kept her on the payroll for themselves and any member of their team. They knew she was the best and deserved to be paid.

"So about that water?" Elijah sat back in his chair and smiled at the agent who rushed out of the room to see what was going on.

******

"Oh my God, Elijah!" Khloé screamed as she jumped in his arms and wrapped her legs around him. He was barely in the door of her condo and she was already on him. Darren and Ace shook their heads as they walked around the couple and went into the living room to sit down. Elijah carried Khloé further into the condo and sat her down on top of the kitchen counter.

"Let me find out you missing a nigga." Elijah smirked. He was happy she was excited to see him. It meant he still had a chance with her.

"Shut up." Khloé said looking down at the floor.

"It's cool, ma." Elijah said lifting her head back up. He placed a kiss on her soft lips. He had missed doing that.

"Ahem." Ace cleared his throat causing everybody to laugh. He knew the two had feelings for each other, but that didn't mean he wanted to see them all on each other like that.

Khloé got down from the counter and began moving around the kitchen to cook dinner for the guys. Elijah walked over to the couch and sat down. He noticed his face all over the TV in the background. He could only imagine what was being said about him. He had worked hard to maintain his image as a successful businessman and rapper. He couldn't let what was happening affect his reputation. He needed these charges dropped ASAP.

"So what you find out?" Darren asked Ace.

"They have an informant. There was no name listed, but I got a guy working on getting his information for you all. He gave them information on your shipments and everything. They had a warrant to search your office and residence as well. Lucky for you that condo was empty, but they're going to be watching you, so be careful about where you go. They have your shipments, but they can't really tie those to you directly. Right now they're going to be on a scramble to find evidence." Ace warned Elijah.

"So you saying I can't go back home?" Elijah asked. Hotel security sucked at keeping the paparazzi out, and he didn't really feel like paying security to follow him everywhere. He moved solo and hated entourages.

"To your townhouse? No. Send Khloé to get what you need." Ace told him seriously. That house was under a different name and the Feds couldn't touch it for now. If they followed him there and found out he lived there, they might be able to get a warrant to search it.

"You can stay here." Khloé offered while placing the food in front of the guys. She had just made some wings and fries.

"Word?" Elijah asked with his eyebrow raised. Was Khloé inviting him into her house… into her bedroom?

"On the couch." Khloé added before walking away.

Elijah twisted his face all up at her last comment. On the couch? Nah. She was tripping if she thought he was sleeping on the damn couch. Darren shook his head. He already knew what Elijah was thinking. Ace chose to stay out of it. Khloé was grown and unless she asked for help, he wouldn't step in.

******

It had been a week since Elijah was released, and he didn't know if he could take being held up in the house anymore. Khloé had gone back to school this week, so she was never around. Kai was evil and pregnant. She asked him a million times a day about Darren. He felt bad for her, but couldn't give up any info on his boy. If Darren wanted to talk to her, he'd answer the phone.

"When your sister supposed to be back?" Elijah asked Kai. It was going on 9 and Khloé hadn't returned home from school yet.

"I don't know." Kai lied. Elijah could see right through the bullshit. He walked away from her and into Khloé's room before slamming the door shut. Kai hurried and texted her sister to let her know Elijah was looking for her.

It was past midnight when Khloé snuck in the apartment door quietly. She breathed a sigh of relief as all the lights were turned off. She knew everyone was sleeping. She hoped she could just make it to her shower and climb into bed before Elijah noticed the time. Her plans were stopped before she could even get 5 steps inside. The living room lamp came on and there sat Elijah smoking on a blunt. The look in his eyes scared her.

"What the—" Khloé grabbed her chest. She was expecting him to just be sitting there waiting on her.

"You know the time?" Elijah said getting up and moving towards her. He was standing before her in the blink of an eye. "Where the fuck you been, Khloé?"

"You can't—" Khloé started to say when Elijah snatched her up by the arm.

"I can't what?" He challenged her.

"You can't question me. You're not my man." Khloé replied, her voice cracking. She wanted to curse herself for not sounding as confident as she wanted to.

"Hm. Is that right?" Elijah questioned her. "That's how you feel?"

"Yeah." Khloé said shaking her arm free. She still didn't sound confident.

"Aight, bet. You got that." Elijah said before grabbing her keys off the counter. If that's how she wanted to play it. She had him all the way fucked up. He slammed the door on his way out causing a picture to fall off the wall and break.

Khloé leaned against the wall and broke down. Kai came out from her room. She had heard everything that just happened. She didn't know why Khloé was trying to play herself. She knew her twin wanted Elijah back. Kai didn't understand. She would give anything to be back with Darren at this moment.

Without saying a word, Kai helped her sister up from the floor and walked her to her room. Khloé lay across with her clothes still on. Kai took off her shoes then turned out the light. They would talk tomorrow.

Chapter 25

Khloé stood in the middle of her lab. She hadn't been here in months. She began walking around the equipment and pulling off their covers. Once upon a time she had found sanctuary in this room trying to make her mark on the medical field. She had a million brilliant ideas that she'd been dying to test, but feared the outcome.

She hated that Blue Wave had cost her friendship with Jesse and her sister to be kidnapped. While originally all she had ever wanted to do was create medicine that didn't have the horrible side effects of modern medicine and would be affordable to those without proper medical coverage, all she had done was create a recreational drug. Khloé pulled out her old journal and began flipping through all the formulas and ideas she had yet to try out. She had already vowed to never make another Blue Wave, but nothing was stopping her from getting back to her original plans of making medicine.

Flipping through her pages, she came across a page with a formula for a medicine that could mimic the effects of Adderall (a pill commonly used to treat those with ADHD), but have a cheaper production cost. Deciding there would be no harm in making such a pill, she set out to work. She pulled out everything she would need and thankfully no one had touched any of her ingredients or equipment. She turned on her Pandora app and got to work.

Three hours later, Khloé had finally created about 20 of the pills. She didn't want to test it on herself, but she couldn't go out and just ask someone to try it for her either. She began to feel defeated, like maybe this was all a waste of time. She put the pills in a little plastic baggy and began clearing up the rest of her mess. She was set to start pharmacy school at Emory in just a few short weeks. The drug world was no place for her.

"What you doing here?" Elijah asked out of nowhere causing Khloé to jump back from being scared.

"Oh my God! Why would you do that?" Khloé said holding her chest. She didn't hear him come in the door or walk up.

"You need to cut that music down. It's not safe for you to be here alone and not be aware of what's going on around you." Elijah said with concern written all over his face. Anybody could run in here and kill her. No one would ever know.

"Why are you here?" Khloé asked. Elijah hadn't been there since Khloé decided to shut it down.

"I was coming through to get pictures of the equipment. I was going to ask what you wanted to do, but I was most likely going to sell all this." Elijah explained.

Khloé didn't know what to say. This lab was more than perfect. It was all hers. She had dreamt it all up herself and

Elijah had helped make it a reality. She was definitely going to be mad to see it go.

"You can sell it." Khloé said sadly. "It's just not the same."

"What's this?" Elijah asked picking up the baggy of pills Khloé had just finished making.

"I don't know. Something I was just messing around with. I don't know if they work or not." Khloé shrugged. She was really having no desire to form a trial or anything. The fun in making medicine might have been taken away from her. Her whole life she knew she would be a part of the medical field, and she thought she had found her calling. She was wrong. The only thing that came from her experiment was heartache and pain. She couldn't go through losing someone close to her ever again.

"What's it do?" Elijah asked.

Though Blue Wave was a partial motivation for Kai's kidnapping, it had done numbers on the street. He had pill poppers asking for it all day long. He would never force Khloé into making it for him. Her twin had been caught up in some drama that had been reignited by that pill hitting the streets.

"It's like Adderall. It is prescribed for people with ADHD, but it helps with focus and concentration." Khloé explained. Elijah's mind was already racing. This pill was actually legal. He was a hustler at heart, so he couldn't help but want to see what it would do on the streets.

"No." Khloé said as she continued to wipe down the counter. She was no longer in the drug business. She was putting her foot down.

"You don't even know what I was going to say." Elijah chuckled.

"Mhm." Khloé said and continued to clean up the space. "So when you getting rid of it?"

Elijah pocketed the baggy of drugs and watched her ass jiggle as she moved around the lab. Khloé was thick as hell. He didn't want to answer her question. He had to get someone to try out her new pills and come up with a way to convince her to make more if these were legit.

"You want to keep it? I won't sell it if you want it." He said instead.

Khloé's eyes lit up as she thought about what he was saying. It had been her dream to have her own lab. Maybe she could find something more productive to do with the space. Like skin and hair treatments. Pills were too dangerous for her. She needed a few more machines, but that seemed like a better idea.

Elijah waited for her to finish cleaning before he locked up and they went their separate ways.

Chapter 26

Khloé looks confused as Ivy drags his bags into their living room behind Kai. She hoped like hell that Kai hadn't invited Ivy to live with them. Ivy was fun, but she wasn't sure she could take his flamboyance all day every day. The last time she had seen him was at their slumber party.

"Come on, hunny. You know the drill. Your man sent the glam squad. You shouldn't even be shocked anymore. Get up and go wash your ass, so I can make you fabulous." Ivy said pulling Khloé off the couch and giving her a hug.

Khloé looked behind him and sure enough there was Jazzy rolling in a rack of clothes. There was more than enough clothes on it. Surely Elijah hadn't sent all of this for her.

"You too, Miss Kai." Jazzy said before walking out the door and rolling in another rack of clothes. Both twins had identical looks of shock on their face.

"Huh?" Kai said sure she hadn't heard Jazzy right.

"If you can huh you can hear." Ivy said setting up his station at his usual spot on the end of the breakfast bar in their kitchen. "Now go."

Khloé and Kai both went to their bedrooms to do as they said and shower. Thirty minutes later they both came out freshly showered and with wet hair.

"I swear I'm going to snag me a baller tonight." Ivy said looking through the racks of clothes trying to see if there was anything he wanted to steal.

"What's going on?" Kai asked Jazzy as she sat in the chair first for Ivy to do her hair and makeup. Since she was pregnant and would be harder to fit, Jazzy wanted to be able to try clothes on her as Khloé got ready.

"Can't say." Jazzy said with a huge smile on her face. She had been sworn to secrecy by Elijah. She was happy her boss was finally going after a good girl and not the usual thots he normally had hanging around.

"Aww." Khloé and Kai said at the same time with identical pouts. Ivy and Jazzy couldn't help but to laugh. They didn't even realize they did it at the same time.

"You been working out?" Jazzy asked Khloé as she watched her try on two different outfits. Khloé's body was beautiful. Both twins wore their weight very well. All the curves were in the right places. Women paid good money for bodies like Khloé's and Kai's.

"Yeah." Khloé said frowning her face up thinking about Malik. He had been too quiet ever since she told him she just wanted to stay friends. She had been working out with him twice a week before he just up and disappeared. She made a note to call him when she got back from wherever Elijah was kidnapping her to.

"You know what you should wear…" Jazzy said going into Khloé's closet after the third outfit she'd tried on didn't work. She pulled the nude jumpsuit that was one of the choices for Khloé's first date with Elijah. "I think this would be a good one. Sex it up a little bit. Show him what he's been missing."

Khloé smiled. This was exactly what she needed. She was tired of everyone seeing her as Miss Innocent. She would put on her grown woman sexy. She was turning 22 in a few hours and was ready to break out of the little girl image people saw her as.

Taking Khloé's smile as confirmation, Jazzy then went to picking out her accessories. She went in her bag and pulled out the gold cuff bracelets Elijah had bought for Khloé. She paired the jumpsuit with some gold pumps and gold accessories. She and Khloé then went back into the living room and sipped on wine as Ivy finished Kai's hair.

An hour later, all three girls and Ivy were ready to go. Kai was dressed in a flowy sheer black dress that fit loosely over her huge baby bump. Ivy had pulled her hair up into a perfect bun on top of her head.

Khloé's jumpsuit looked painted on. She was sure to turn every head tonight. Ivy had curled her hair and beat her face to perfection. She felt confident and couldn't wait for Elijah to see her.

******

"SURPRISE!" The whole club shouted as the girls walked through the door. They both broke out in big smiles as they saw their men approaching them.

Kai had been hesitant to get out the car seeing that they had pulled up to the club. She had vowed to never be pregnant and in the club, but seeing Darren standing before her with a smile on his face, none of that mattered anymore.

"And the birthday girls just walked in… Shout out to Khloé and Kai on their 22nd! Turn up ladies!" The DJ shouted and began playing music. The club went back to normal as the crowd went back to drinking and dancing.

Elijah led Khloé by the hand up to their VIP section. He and Darren had bought out every section just for their party. The whole VIP was theirs and all drinks were also on him until 1 am. It had cost him a good amount of money, but he didn't care. He'd make it all back in a day or so. He'd do anything to put the smile on her face like the one that Khloé currently wore. When they got upstairs, they posed for a few pictures before he pulled her over to one of the sofas and down on his lap.

"Why you got all my ass on display like that?" He whispered in her ear causing her to blush. "If another nigga look too hard, you gon' make me catch a body in here."

Khloé giggled and then pushed his hand off her butt. She then turned and asked the waitress to get her a drink. Darren and Elijah had paid two of the bartenders to exclusively wait on their section for the night. They also had personal waitresses as well.

"I'm for real, ma. You looking good as hell." Elijah said returning his hand to her ass. Khloé looked good as hell. He loved the fact that she wasn't conceited and blushed at his every compliment. She paid no attention to all the women trying to grab his attention or the million camera flashes going off around them. Her attention was 100% focused on her man.

Khloé had already consumed two very strong drinks. She knew she was tipsy by the way she kept giggling and watching Elijah. She had been dancing in front of him and on his lap all night. Feeling extremely confident from all the attention and compliments she was receiving, she bent forward and kissed him on the lips. Their tongues swirled together as Elijah deepened the kiss. They looked like a bunch of teenagers who couldn't keep their hands off of each other. They were finally in a good space and both were secretly hoping it lasted.

Across the table there was a lot of tension between Kai and Darren. They hadn't spoken since he had caught her out with Eric. This party had already been planned and she deserved it. That was the only reason he'd gone through with it. He had to admit that she looked good as hell in her dress. The pregnancy had her honey colored skin glowing flawlessly. He watched over her and made sure the waitress only bought her juice and virgin drinks all night. Kai was growing tired of the silent treatment. She got up and sat on Darren's lap.

"You gon' be mad at me forever, daddy?" Kai pouted as she began giving him a lap dance. She could see in his face, he was trying to hold strong as he nodded, but the way his erection began hardening beneath her spoke otherwise. His eyes held nothing but lust as he watched her dance on him. The look in his eyes would have her panties soaked, if she was wearing any.

Darren pulled his fitted hat down over his eyes a little more. He couldn't resist the urge to kiss her lips as she pouted. Her lips looked glossy and juicy as she pouted. He was on brick instantly as he remembered how good they felt wrapped around his 9 inches. He was mad at her, though, so he wouldn't be going there with her tonight. He picked her up and placed her back on the sofa.

Kai couldn't believe he had just dissed her like that. She got up to run to the bathroom before the tears could fall from her eyes. She hated that pregnancy had her crying. Any other time she would have went off on him, but she didn't want to give him the satisfaction of seeing her cry. She also didn't want to ruin Khloé's night. She could tell her sister was enjoying being around Elijah again and looked genuinely happy.

Khloé got up to go after her sister, but Elijah held her back.

"Let them handle their business. That ain't got shit to do with us." He said in her ear.

A few seconds later, Darren stood and followed behind Kai. He hated to see her cry. He had wanted to hurt her like she'd hurt him, but seeing the look on her face proved it wasn't worth it. He pushed the door, but she had already locked it. He figured she must be in there alone. He knocked on the bathroom door hoping she would just open it up. She wouldn't open it if she knew it was him on the other side. Kai was very stubborn.

Kai stood at the sink and wiped her eyes. She ignored the knocks at the door, they could wait. Why would he invite her out tonight only to treat her like shit and embarrass her? She felt like this would be a good time to move on from their issues. Her baby would be here in a little over a month, and she didn't want to bring him into the world with his possible father being mad at her. If Darren wanted to be mad at her, then he should have stayed away from her like he had been doing.

She heard the locks starting to click. She rolled her eyes and wiped the runny mascara from her cheeks before she came face to face with those hazel eyes she fell in love with. She quickly gazed down at the floor not wanting to give in to him.

"I'm sorry." He said. Kai could see the apology in his eyes, but she wasn't ready to forgive him. She just turned and continue to primp herself in the mirror, laying down the invisible stray hairs in her perfectly laid bun that sat atop her head. She felt his hardness press into her backside but she still didn't give him any eye contact. She hadn't had sex since their split and she was horny as hell, but she wasn't about to go there with him.

"You hear me?" Darren said lowly. He pressed himself into her once more before placing kisses on her neck. He reached around her and began massaging her breasts. They had gotten so much bigger with her pregnancy. He could tell they were really swollen tonight.

"Stop." Kai whispered. She didn't really want him to stop. She knew he wouldn't. They way her body responded to his touch was so natural. She couldn't stay mad at him if she wanted to, especially with him touching her in that way.

Darren ignore her as he began lifting up the back of her dress. He was excited and angry at the same time that she wasn't wearing any panties.

"You just knew you was getting some, huh?" He said as he pushed two fingers inside her dripping love tunnel.

"Mmmm." Kai couldn't form words. She leaned her head back and stared at his dark, lust filled, hazel eyes in the mirror.

He used two fingers and penetrated her love tunnel. He moved in and out of her at a slow pace. The faces she was making as he watched her in the mirror had his dick trying to break out the front of his jeans. He used his free hand to reach down and undo his pants, never breaking the rhythm he had going inside her. His hand was soaked from her juices running out of her.

"Damn. Ooooooh!" Kai moaned as he invaded her. It had been a minute since he had been inside of her and there was a mixture of pain and pleasure as he tried to force all of him inside her. She was so tight. She pushed back on him trying to get him further in her, but he pulled back.

"How many times daddy have to tell you. You not running shit." Darren said pulling out of her. He could see the frustration in her face as she tooted her ass up at him, begging with her eyes in the mirror for him to enter her once again.

"Please." She begged, her eyes an intense dark gray color. It was sexy as fuck to him that her eyes changed colors with her mood. He thrust all the way into her, causing her to gasp.

"This what you wanted, huh?" He began stroking her harder. There were people starting to knock on the door, but he had to make sure she got her nut. He knew Kai liked it a little rough. She put both hands on the countertop as he got a steady rhythm and moved in and out of her. She met him thrust for thrust. She could feel her orgasm building up inside of her. Darren felt how slippery she was getting, he knew she was getting close. He wrapped his arm around her waist so she wouldn't fall.

"Cum for daddy, ma." He whispered in her ear before biting her earlobe between his teeth.

"OH FUCK!" Kai screamed out as she came. Darren exploded inside her as he came with her. Darren held onto her until her body stopped shaking from her orgasm.

Kai's cheeks blushed red at the realization of what they'd just done. She hoped the music was loud enough outside that no one had heard her. They cleaned each other off with paper towels and wipes from Kai's clutch. They shared a passionate kiss before walking out the bathroom hand in hand ignoring the angry and knowing looks from everyone waiting.

******

Khloé looked around the club for Elijah. She had been wrapped up in a conversation with Jazzy about school when he disappeared. She couldn't find him anywhere and hoped he wasn't somewhere with some girl. She had decided to give him one last chance and would be done with him for good if he was up to his same old bullshit. She cursed Kai under her breath for also abandoning her. She knew her twin was off somewhere hooking up with Darren. They were so cute how they played mad at each other knowing they were just going to make up.

Khloé laughed as she watched Kai half limp back to the VIP couches. She was about to make fun of Kai when the music stopped and Elijah's voice came over the speakers. She got up and walked to the railing that overlooked the rest of the club. A spotlight shone down on Elijah where he stood in the middle of the dancefloor and he began to speak.

"I ain't good with this speech shit so work with a nigga." Elijah said causing the crowd to laugh a little. "Today is the birthday of a girl very special to me. I been fucking up ever since I met her and somehow she ain't beat a nigga ass yet. She up there looking good as hell right now. I want to see her sexy ass all day every day. She been silently rocking with your boy even though we ain't made shit official yet. So I'm going to ask right here on stage in front of all these strange ass mufuckas. Give me another chance, ma. I'm gon' get it right this time."

There were a bunch of "awws" as he finished his speech. Suddenly the crowd then went wild as Fetty Wap appeared next to Elijah and began to sing.

'I want you to be mine again, baby. I know my lifestyle is driving you crazy. I cannot see myself without you. We call them fans though, girl you know how we do. I go out of my way to please you. I go out of my way to see you'

Khloé couldn't help the smile that covered her face as she watched Elijah perform

alongside Fetty Wap. When the song finished, Fetty Wap started another song while Elijah made his way up to Khloé, where she stood still blushing and feeling shy that all eyes were on her. He stood behind as she looked over the railing and watched Fetty continue to perform. Elijah whispered the words in her ears. He had gone all out for her birthday and she couldn't wait to thank him later.

Chapter 27

"Slow down shawty." Jacob said as he watched Camryn do another line.

He had found her working in The Pink Pony strip club out in Forest Park. It was a giant step down from her usual job at Magic City. She had gotten kicked out of there because of her constant drug use. The owners didn't care what you did before or after you left the club, but they had a strict no drug on site policy for all the girls. She had been caught twice by security doing lines of coke in the dressing room.

The Pink Pony wasn't a bad spot. The problem was that the clientele was mostly white or really young. She made good tips, but it was nothing compared to what she was pulling in at Magic City. She was about to give up and go begging for her job back when in walked Jacob. He had on so much jewelry, she had been temporarily blinded by it when the lights hit him. He was the sexiest man to enter the establishment since she'd been working there.

"Fuck!" Cam shouted as her nose began to bleed and dripped into the small mountain of coke she had sitting on the edge of the coffee table.

"Bae, I been thinking. We need to make a move on your ex. I know you say he the good guy now, but in order for us to take over Atlanta, we got to start making moves." Jacob coaxed her as she returned from the bathroom with a towel over her face.

Camryn listened to what Jacob was saying. She didn't really care about taking over Atlanta or bringing down Darren. She hadn't even thought about seeing her kids in months. Since a week ago, when she met Jacob, he had been supplying her with endless amounts of coke. All she wanted to do was get high and go to the club to make her money. The only thing she needed him for was drugs and sex when she got high and horny. He was the one who kept mentioning this great takeover plan.

Jacob was starting to see that Camryn was only into the drugs. All day long she slept and did lines, then returned to the club at night. She didn't cook or clean. He had told her he would take care of her, but she said she enjoyed the rush of dancing. Jacob didn't care what she enjoyed. After he got what he needed from her, he didn't care what happened to her, so her dancing wasn't that bad. Camryn was the sexiest woman he'd ever been with, but her drug use wasn't a good look for the future King of Atlanta.

Seeing that Camryn wasn't about to make any real moves, he called up an old friend of his father's in the FBI and set up another meeting.

"I got an errand to run. Don't try and stuff all that shit up your nose." Jacob threw to Cam as he left out of the house. He knew his warning would fall on deaf ears.

******

An hour later, Jacob valeted his car and walked into Ray's on the River in Sandy Springs. He told the hostess he was meeting someone, and she led the way to the table where the agent sat. Sam Lynch was a fat white man standing 5'8 and 275 lbs. He had greasy graying hair and cold blue eyes. His whole demeanor screamed crooked cop. Jacob's father, Sean, had used Sam's services more than once to keep himself and Dame out of prison. Jacob was meeting with him to help with the take down of Elijah's empire.

"What's good?" Jacob said shaking Sam's hand before he took a seat in the booth.

"So, your boys Elijah Williams and Darren Price have someone working for them on the inside. Elijah was able to make bail. Somehow the evidence we planted against him came up missing. His lawyer was able to get the case dismissed. You need to give me something harder to stick him with." Sam said. Jacob didn't know it, but Sam had a personal vendetta against Elijah. When he and Darren expanded their business to Atlanta, they had refused to pay Sam his percentage to sell their drugs on what he considered his streets. In fact, Elijah had laughed at him and told Sam he didn't know what the fuck he was talking about.

"I don't know what else to do. Nyah ain't giving up shit either." Jacob said. He had been trying to get Nyah in on his plans. She said she was working on some other stuff and "didn't have time for his bullshit ass plans". He only asked her because he figured that he could watch her more closely, but so far it hasn't been working out that way. Nyah was up to something and he wanted to know what.

"Well what the fuck are we meeting for?" Sam stood up. He was disappointed in the young man. His father, Sean, had helped Sam put away many men and even paid him nicely. So far all Jacob had been giving him is a bunch of empty promises. "Don't call me until you have something that sticks." Sam said before turning to leave.

Jacob sat for a minute trying to come up with a new plan. He needed to force Camryn into action somehow. All she did was sit and snort up all his coke. Maybe if he cut off her supply, she'd be more willing to help. He got up and threw a couple of bills on the table before he left. Whether she knew it or not, Camryn was about to help him set up her baby-daddy.

******

"So all you want me to do is knock on the door?" Camryn asked again as they drove closer to the house she once shared with Darren. She pulled down the sun visor mirror to check out her appearance. It had been months since she had ran into Darren or seen her kids, she didn't want to scare him away.

"No, shawty. I need you to work your way back into his good graces. Just ask him to come home and play the good wife for a while. Then invite me over one day while he's at work." Jacob reminded her. He was growing frustrated with her. They had gone over the plan about ten times since he'd picked her up from his house.

"It's right up here." Camryn pointed at the house up ahead. Jacob slowed down and pulled into the driveway. "What the fuck?"

Jacob climbed out of the car behind Camryn. He hoped she hadn't brought him to the wrong house. This one was clearly empty and up for sale. Camryn walked up to the front door and lifted up the little flower pot. The spare key was even gone. She couldn't believe he had up and left and took her kids. What did he do with all her stuff? She stormed off back to the car and climbed in the driver's seat. What the fuck was going on with Darren?

Jacob noticed the change in her attitude. Maybe her seeing her old house like this was the push she needed to jump onboard with his plans. He went around the car to get in. His door was barely closed as she pulled out the driveway. She sped out of the neighborhood.

"Where you going? You might want to slow down before you attract 12." Jacob asked her. She'd been driving for about 10 minutes and only seemed to be speeding up.

"I got this don't worry." Cam snapped. She was agitated. She loved that house. She hadn't even been gone for a year and Darren was already moving on. While he was away, she kept that house clean from top to bottom and raised his kids.

For three years she kept money on his books and spent all day Saturday bringing their kids to visit him. He hadn't even given her the courtesy of a phone call. He had life fucked up.

Jacob looked up as they pulled up in front of a huge glass building in North Atlanta. Cam had parked very crookedly in a spot before jumping out, leaving the door open and car running. He hoped like hell she didn't go in there causing a scene and running off her ex.

"Can I help you?" Darren's secretary asked Camryn with her nose turned up. Camryn was dressed in some ripped jeans and a cut off shirt that revealed the bottom of her breasts. Her nose was running and her hair was all over her head. She couldn't even stand still.

"I'm here to see Darren Price. Tell him his wife is here." Camryn looked at the girl up and down. She was very young and attractive. She was dressed professionally but still sexy. Camryn wondered if Darren had been sleeping with her.

"Camryn… What are you doing here?" Darren came out behind his secretary.

"YOU SOLD MY HOUSE, DARREN!" She screamed at him causing everyone in the lobby area to stop and stare.

"What the fuck is your problem, yo?" He said grabbing her by the arm and pulling her into his office. "You left me and your kids almost a year ago and now you showing up to my job high as hell and looking a hot ass mess for what?"

Camryn could see the look of disgust on Darren's face. His hazel eyes which used to look at her with such love showed nothing. He didn't love her anymore and the realization hit her in the gut like a ton of bricks.

"I came by to see you. I wanted to see my kids." Camryn stuttered. "I'm going to get clean for you all. I want my family back."

Darren didn't believe a word she was saying. Someone who wanted help would not be standing in front of him with glossy eyes and a runny nose. When he met Camryn she was doing drugs. The only reason she'd stopped is because he babysat her every day of her pregnancy. When he went to prison she had to stay sober for the children. The first thing she did when he got out of prison was abandon all her responsibilities and go back to that life. Just looking at her, he could tell she wasn't the same person. She had lost weight and her hair hadn't been washed in weeks, it looks like.

The Camryn he knew cared more about her looks than anything. She was not afraid to use her good looks to get whatever she wanted. So she kept her body right and stayed getting her hair and nails done every week. It hurt him to see her this way, but she had made her own decisions. His kids had a new woman in their lives and rarely asked for their mother. What did she expect?

"Are you listening to me? I want us to be like we used to." Camryn said coming around his desk and attempting to sit on it looking sexy.

"I hear you. Get clean and then we'll talk." Darren said dismissing her. He could tell what she was trying to do, but it wasn't working. He looked over her once voluptuous body and shook his head. Her once round bottom had lost some of its curve. Her sitting up on his desk only showed her weight loss and sickened him more.

"You're kicking me out?" She asked shockingly. Darren could never refuse her. She had been away too long or maybe he had someone else. Someone like his cute secretary. "Are you fucking her?"

"Who?" Darren's head shot up at her accusation.

"Mr. Price, your 4 o'clock is here." The secretary's voice came over the intercom.

"HER! You're fucking your fucking secretary! Is that it? Is that why you sold my fucking house? You want to be with that bitch!" Camryn stood up and started poking her finger in Darren's face as she yelled.

"Yo, get your fucking hand out my face. Don't come in here being disrespectful. Who I fuck is none of your concern anymore. You lost all that when you abandoned *my* fucking kids!" Darren spoke harshly, his voice loud and full of bass. He was trying not to cause a scene in his office, but Cam was begging to get choked. Her mouth was always disrespectful.

"Nah, don't try and put this on me! You were already working late before I left for some me time. You were probably already fucking this bitch!" She snapped back.

Just then there was a loud knock on the door. Darren got up to open it and in walked security followed by his secretary.

Darren went and sat back behind his desk. He'd let them handle it. He was done arguing with her.

"Ma'am, we're going to have to ask you to leave." One of the men spoke.

"So you just going to let your little bitch kick me out?" Camryn turned and asked Darren. When he didn't say anything, she tried to rush over to him and slap him, but security grabbed her.

"This how you gon' do me! I'm the mother of your kids!" Cam kicked and screamed as security dragged her out of the building. "You stupid mother fucker! I'm coming for my kids!"

Security set her outside the door as she continued to scream. They stood on the other side of the door waiting for her to leave. She screamed a couple more obscenities before walking off to where Jacob was parked.

"What the fuck happened?" Jacob said as she climbed in the passenger seat.

"He'll come around." Camryn said simply as she pulled down the visor and began messing with her hair. She was going to get her shit together and take back what was rightfully hers. Darren thought shit was sweet because she was away, but he was about to feel her presence.

Jacob shook his head and pulled off back towards his house. He could see the crazed look in her eyes. Maybe fucking with Camryn wasn't a good idea.

Chapter 28

Nyah jumped up and reached for her gun. Heavy footsteps approaching her bed had waken her from her sleep

"Calm down." Olivia said bringing in some food for Nyah. The two of them had been hiding out in upstate New York ever since Olivia's run in with Ace at the hotel.

Nyah got up and went to the bathroom. She had no words for her mother. She knew Olivia had planned to leave her at the cemetery. Nyah didn't understand why Olivia was trying to play mother of the year now. As she brushed her teeth she counted the number of times she had seen her mother over the years. Olivia had never once cooked a meal for her, brushed her hair, or worried about her safety. She was up to something and Nyah couldn't wait to find out what it was.

"You're not going to eat?" Olivia asked pointing at the tray of food she had brought up to Nyah's room. She had made fried chicken wings, baked macaroni and cheese, greens, and cornbread; Nyah's favorite. She watched as Nyah walked through the room looking for stuff for her shower. She got up and walked out leaving the food when Nyah walked in the bathroom and locked the door without a word.

"Daddy, why Mommy don't love me?" A 12-year-old Nyah asked her father.

"Mommy loves you. She just has a different way of showing it." Dame replied. He too was growing tired of Olivia and all her excuses. It had been years since Ace left and it was clear he wasn't returning. It was time Olivia put forth more of an effort to spend time with their daughter.

"She don't love me. She doesn't act like it. She never spends time with me. She doesn't do my hair, pick out my clothes, or talk to me. All she does is get mad when I talk to her." Nyah said looking sad.

It pained Dame to see his daughter speak about her mother that way. He no longer cared about getting back at Ace or convincing Olivia to love him, but he needed her to spend more time with Nyah. It was unfair to the child to know her mother and not feel love.

"I'll make sure she comes and spends time with you. Have a fun girls' day. Would you like that, baby girl?" Dame asked trying to cheer her up.

"No sir. She won't do it. I don't want to get my hopes up." Nyah turned and went to her room.

Nyah let her tears mix with the water as she rinsed the shampoo from her hair. She had cut her weave out and let her natural hair flow. She was thinking about changing it again, so Elijah wouldn't notice her. Then a part of her felt like she should just take all the money including the insurance money her father had left her and leave the country. Anything was better than living here and pretending to be one of her sisters' friends. Sisters she never knew she had and knew nothing about her.

"Nyah, honey, I'm going to the mall. You want to come?" Olivia asked from the other side of the bathroom door.

Nyah ignored her and continued to wash her body. She was starting to feel like it was a mistake coming here. When Olivia had first asked her to come to New York with her for a while until things died out, Nyah saw it as a chance to spend time with her mother for the first time ever. When they arrived and Olivia introduced her to Gregg as one of Kai's friends, Nyah knew Olivia was full of shit. Her first thought was to walk out of the door and take her chances back in Atlanta, but that part of her that still wanted her mother's love kept her here. Something in her was telling her Olivia was forcing herself to spend time with her.

Growing up, Nyah would have given anything for her mother to cook her meals or do her hair. Now she felt like Olivia was just doing it to keep up a good front for her husband. Nyah was just a pawn in Olivia's game. She was starting to feel like her father had done her the same way. Nyah wasn't sure what it was about Ace, but he had her mother and father doing real evil things to get back at him.

******

"How much longer is she going to be here, Olivia?" Gregg asked his wife as she sat on the edge of their bed applying lotion to her body. He didn't believe a word she'd said about the girl being a friend of her daughters'. He could count on one hand how many times he'd seen Khloé and Kai since they'd gotten married, and now Olivia was bringing home one of their friends that she'd known since she was a child? There was just no way. Plus Nyah looked exactly like his wife. Those grey eyes were rare, especially on a black woman.

"For a while. She was in a bad situation back home and she's waiting it out. If it's too much, hun, I'll ask her to leave." Olivia said faking an attitude. She knew Gregg hated to argue and would agree with her just off that fact alone.

"Okay." Gregg said before cutting off the lamp on his side of the bed and getting comfortable.

Olivia looked back at her husband of the last 5 years and smirked. She knew exactly what he needed to get him back on her side. Gregg was a handsome older man. At 52 years old, he still had the body of a 35 year old. He was 5'11 and had milk chocolate skin. His hair was a good mix of black and gray. He reminded her of the actor from the Allstate commercials. She turned off the light on her side of the bed before wrapping her arm around her husband.

"Not tonight." Gregg said before pushing away her hand. He knew exactly what she was trying to do, and he wasn't going to allow for it. Olivia thought he was oblivious to her random trips and the fact that she'd been married four times before. He'd hired a private investigator to look into her and discovered a lot of things about her that he didn't like.

Olivia was shocked by him turning her away. He had never one time denied her sex. She was rarely home and when she returned, he was always like a horny teenager. They would be holed up for hours making love. Something was off about him this time she returned. She hoped it had nothing to do with Nyah. That girl was always ruining something for her. Olivia would deal with it tomorrow. Instead of putting up a fight like she normally would, she turned over and tried to go to sleep.

******

It had been a week since Nyah left her mother's house. She decided to take her chances back in Atlanta. She had rented a townhouse under another fake name on the south side of Atlanta in Jonesboro. The complex was gated and had an actual security guard to check in visitors. She could move around her place without being afraid of someone finding her. She rolled her eyes as she ignored yet another phone call from Olivia.

Nyah had tried to stay with her mother, but the constant reminder of what Olivia wasn't to her was too much to bear. Nyah could see that Olivia was trying to form a bond with her, but maybe it was too late. In the back of her mind, something was telling Nyah that Olivia had an ulterior motive for being nice to her. In 19 years, Olivia had never once tried to form a relationship with her. Half the time she showed up only to stop the calls from Dame. She never even spent time with Nyah. She'd argue with Dame and then leave. When Nyah was 15, Olivia stopped coming by altogether.

"Daddy, do you think mom will make it?" A 15-year-old Nyah asked her father.

Dame didn't answer. He didn't want to lie to her or break her heart. He knew how Nyah felt about her mother. A part of him felt like it was his own fault since he'd been the one to beg Olivia not to have the abortion.

Nyah could see the hesitation in her father's face. Instead of asking him again she turned away and went into the basement where Dame had set up a personal gun range for her. She loaded her weapon, placed on the safety goggles and ear muffs, then began shooting rounds at the paper target. Tears burned her eyes, but she wouldn't let them fall. She was turning 16 tomorrow, she was practically a woman. It was time to get over her issues with her mother. Olivia clearly didn't give a damn about her, so she wouldn't give a damn about Olivia.

Dame watched his daughter from the doorway of the room. He was frustrated because there was nothing he could do to take away her pain. Olivia didn't even care to know the hell she was putting their child through. If she were around today, Dame would probably put a bullet in her his damn self. He was so wrapped in his own thoughts, he didn't even hear the gunshots stop.

"It's okay, Daddy. She obviously has something more important to do." Nyah said. She gave her father a hug before telling him good-night and going to her room. Tomorrow was her Sweet 16 party and her mother wouldn't be there. It was bad enough Olivia had stood her up when they were supposed to go shopping for an outfit. Instead Olivia had sent a dress by messenger and said it would be perfect for her. The dress was two sizes too small.

Nyah cried herself to sleep that night. When she woke up the next morning she pushed all thoughts of having a relationship with her mother to the back of her head. She closed her heart to Olivia and everyone else.

Nyah reached for her gun. She thought she'd heard something coming from downstairs. She made sure there were bullets before screwing on the silencer. She crept down the stairs with the gun in front of her. She wasn't taking any chances. Shoot first ask questions later. As she stepped foot on the bottom step, she thought she heard a noise coming from her back door. She went in the kitchen and grabbed a knife. Clutching the knife to her chest, she pushed open the back door and fired a shot. A cat then jumped off her trash can toppling it over and running through the backyard. She laughed at herself for being so scary as she closed the door back.

"This shit has to end." She said to herself as she went in her cabinet and pulled out a bottle of Patron. She got didn't even bother with a glass, not that she had anything. Her temporary home had just the basics. She wasn't much of a cook, so she ate out most of the time. All she had was plastic cups. She took two shots to the head before going to sit on her cheap couch to come up with a plan. She was tired of hiding, she was ready to shake shit up.

Chapter 29

"I have so much work to do it's not even funny. I didn't think school would be this hard." Khloé said as she dug through her cross body MK bag looking for her car keys.

"You'll be fine. You the smartest sexiest nerd I know." Elijah said laughing. "Now hurry up and get home, I have a problem for you to solve."

"You so nasty." Khloé laughed. She unlocked the car door before climbing inside. Her phone automatically connected to the Bluetooth inside the car.

"You like it." Elijah laughed.

Khloé smiled knowing he was right. Since she had broken up with Malik and he stopped messing with that Bria girl, she and Elijah were getting back to normal again. He had pretty much moved into her condo since she refused to go back to his townhouse with him. She felt like he probably had a million girls running through there since their last break up, and she refused to sleep anywhere he'd had sex with someone else. Contrary to what she thought she knew, other than Justice, no one else had ever been inside his home. Elijah used his condo or hotel rooms for that.

"I'll see you when I get home." Khloé said before hanging up.

On the thirty minute drive back to her condo, she thought about the advice Kai had given Jazzy at the slumber party. She wondered if she should do something like that for Elijah. She had been thinking about making things official with him again. They had gone on a bunch of dates and were sharing a space, but she knew she needed to talk to him to make him understand that this was his final chance. She wasn't going back and forth with him about other women or baby-mamas. She hoped like hell whenever Justice returned, she had some act right. That whole baby-mama from hell thing was so played out.

"What in the w—" Khloé said as she walked into her apartment. There were a line of white and pink rose petals and candles leading to her bedroom door. She followed the petals until she reached her bedroom door. On her bed was an ice bucket with a bottle of wine and a silver tray with chocolate covered strawberries and a bowl of peaches. No one had ever done anything like this for her before.

Khloé, you been dealing with my bullshit for a minute. I'm ready to show you that I can be the man you need ma. Give me another chance and I promise to get it right this time. Right now I got something special planned for us. I ran you a hot bath. So go soak and when you come out, I'll be waiting for you.

Elijah

Khloé smiled real big after reading the note. She undressed and pulled her hair up into a ball on the top of her head using a hair tie from her wrist. Walking in the bathroom, she gasped as she noticed more rose petals that led up to the tub and into the water. She threw her dirty clothes in the hamper next to the door. She put a foot in the tub and stepped in. It was the perfect temperature. Elijah had also used her Midnight Pomegranate bubble bath from Bath & Body Works that she liked.

She sat back and relaxed with a glass of wine and wondered where Elijah was hiding. He had done all this and she hadn't seen him when she came inside. His surprise was definitely working and Khloé couldn't wait to show him how much she liked it. She smiled to herself thinking about how much he had changed her; some good and some bad.

"I hope I'm the one bringing you that smile." Elijah said interrupting her thoughts.

Khloé looked up and nodded slowly. Her mouth watered at the sight of him and even though she was in the tub, she could feel herself getting wet. Elijah was standing there shirtless with just a pair of jeans. She unconsciously licked her lips as her eyes went from his handsome face, down his chocolate chest, over his sculpted abs, and landed at the bulge that was growing in his pants.

"See something you like?" He asked with a smirk on his face.

Khloé's whole face blushed red and she looked away from him. When she looked back he was undressing as if he were going to join her. Elijah knew that Khloé was still very inexperienced, but he was having fun teaching her. Her blushing did something to him, he couldn't just stand there watching her anymore. He wanted to climb in and be pressed up against her.

Reading his mind, Khloé moved forward so he could climb in behind her. Usually there was a lot of talking between the two of them, but for some reason she was feeling shy. She laid her head back against his chest thinking this is exactly what she needed. She could feel his hardness pressing into her back. She needed that just as much as he did. Without speaking, she stood and faced him before lowering herself onto his hard 11 inches.

"Ooooh." She moaned out as he completely filled her up inside. No matter how many times they'd had sex, she still had to stop for a moment to adjust to his huge size. After a few moments she began moving herself up and down his length slowly.

Elijah locked eyes with her as she made love to him. He kissed her softly on the lips before probing her mouth with his tongue. He used one of his hands to rub her clit as she moved up and down at her own pace. He loved the feeling of being inside her. There was no other girl that fit him like this. The way her body gripped him with each down stroke had him wanting to moan out like a girl, but he wouldn't. He let her work herself at her own pace until he felt her pussy get real slippery and start to contract around him. He knew she was about to reach her peak. He grabbed onto her and began thrusting upward to meet her halfway.

"Yes! I'm about to cum, baby!" Khloé screamed out.

Elijah thrust up into her harder. The slipperiness of the tub was not allowing him to go as hard as he wanted to. His only mission was making sure she had a good nut. He took one of her nipples in his mouth and sucked gently before biting down on it sending her into orgasmic bliss.

"Yessssss!" Khloé cried out as she came.

She wrapped her arms around his neck and road out her orgasm. Elijah, still hard, was ready for another round. Khloé had woke up the beast, and she was already trying to tap out. Not before he got his and not before she came at least 4 more times. Elijah stood with her wrapped in his strong arms, climbed out the tub, and walked them to the shower.

He turned the showerhead on and walked until Khloé's back was on the wall underneath it. Water poured over both their bodies as he began to move inside of her again. Her walls were slippery and creamy from the orgasm she'd just had. Elijah loved it. He watched his dick go in and out of her with her juices on it.

"Oh my God!" All Khloé could do was moan.

"Damn, ma!" Elijah moaned back. His fingers pressed into her thighs as he thrust in and out of her. He was squeezing hard and she bruised easy. He knew he should let her down, but she was feeling too good to him at the moment. He pounded away into her trying to get her to come with him. When she started calling his name and moaning loudly, he knew she was close. He gave it to her relentlessly.

"Fuck!" He cried out as he exploded inside of her. Khloé came again right after him. Neither one of them caring about the fact that they hadn't used protection, and she wasn't on birth control.

Elijah finally put her down, but Khloé sank to the floor causing Elijah to laugh. Her legs felt like jelly. He knew he had put in that work. After washing himself and her, he again carried her to her bed and stood her next to it. Khloé watched him move around her room picking up random items along the way. He came back with a large towel and dried her off.

Elijah laid her down gently and began rubbing lotion on every part of her body. Khloé was starting to fall asleep from all the attention he was giving her. His strong hands felt good as he massaged her whole body. If it weren't for the two sessions they just had in the bathroom, she might have been up for more. After he was done rubbing her down, Khloé tried to move and get under the blankets but Elijah had other plans for her.

He spread her legs apart and began planting soft kisses between her thighs and around her center. Khloé whimpered as he gave attention everywhere else except where she wanted. Elijah was teasing her and she didn't like it. She moved her hips trying to catch some attention from the fire starting up in her middle. Elijah looked up at her and chuckled. He loved the power he was having over her body. The frustrated look on her face was even sexy.

He stood up and kissed her on the lips. Khloé was mad. She thought he was going to leave her frustrated like this. He handed her a sleep mask and told her to put it on. Hesitantly, she did as he asked and then laid back. Elijah planted soft kisses down her body as he made his way back down to her middle. This time he used his tongue and licked her swollen pearl.

"Mmmmm." Khloé moaned, finally getting what she wanted.

Elijah sucked on her pearl a little before letting his tongue slide in her love tunnel. Khloé began moving her hips again trying to fuck herself on his tongue, but he had other plans. Going back to suck on her clit, he took a peach slice from the bowl and used it to penetrate her. He slid it in and out a few times creating a new sensation for Khloé. Her body couldn't take it anymore and she came again. Elijah latched onto her and sucked her completely dry before feeding the peach to her.

Khloé couldn't believe what he was doing to her. She felt him climb up her body as she uncovered her eyes. Elijah was happy she was hanging in there with him. He knew she'd probably tap out by now. Khloé gazed up into his brown eyes. She could see something in them, but wasn't sure she was ready for all that yet. So much was still up in the air, but she couldn't deny she was feeling it too.

Elijah kissed her passionately as he entered into her again. He grabbed her ankles and pushed them back as far as they could go. Khloé wasn't sure she could take anymore of him tonight. Her body had other plans though as it began to leak out like a broken faucet once again. She tried to push back on his stomach as he drove deeper and deeper into her, but he pushed her hands away. He was very deliberate with his strokes. After about ten minutes, he felt his seeds boiling inside of him. He bit down on his lip as he emptied himself into her once again and let her legs go.

Neither one of them had any energy left, so he just rolled over on his back next to her as they drifted off to sleep.

Chapter 30

"He is so cute! Awww auntie's baby!" Khloé gushed at the sight of Kai's baby.

"Of course he is. He looks just like his daddy." Darren said proudly. He gave Kai a kiss on her forehead. "Thank you, ma." He whispered to her causing her to smile.

Baby Derrick Dominic Price was born 8lbs and 8 oz. He was the spitting image of his father. The moment he opened his hazel eyes confirmed exactly who his father was. Kai went ahead and ordered the DNA test just to be sure. She had told Eric to come up to the hospital tomorrow. She didn't want to create a scene, but she needed him to understand that the baby was not his, and he needed to leave her and her family alone.

Khloé was hogging the baby and wouldn't let anyone hold him. Ace was overjoyed at being a grandpa. He couldn't wait until Derrick was old enough to come visit with him. Dutch had everybody laughing he kept calling the baby "lil nigga" and causing Kai to cuss him out. Zane sat watching the family moment. It made his need for a family grow stronger.

The moment was bittersweet for Elijah. He was happy for his brother, but he was missing his son like crazy. He got up from the chair and stepped outside for a minute. He didn't want his attitude to affect the happy moment negatively.

Khloé saw how down he seemed, so she finally handed the baby over to Ace and followed Elijah out of the room.

"Don't worry. He's going to come back to you." She said wrapping her arms around Elijah's back as he looked out the window at the downtown skyline.

"I just think. I missed his birth. I missed his first words and steps. I know I fucked up with his mother, but that don't mean I should be punished by keeping me away from him."

Khloé agreed with everything he said. She simply laid her face against his back and comforted him. Elijah appreciated her for being there for him while he was upset about another woman. Most girls would be insecure, but Khloé stuck by his side and didn't make a big deal of anything.

"Let's go back in so I can spoil my nephew some more." Khloé said excitedly.

Elijah had to laugh. She hadn't let the baby go since Darren first handed him over. You would think Derrick was her baby by the way she was watching over him. He couldn't wait to pop some babies in her. He could already tell she would make a good mother.

"Well I'm going to get out of here and let you get some rest, baby girl. He's perfect. You did good." Ace was saying to Kai as they walked back in the room hand in hand. He kissed both twins on the forehead and then dapped up Darren, Zane, and Elijah before walking out.

"I'm out too. Can't believe you, lil nigga. I'm too young and fly to be a damn grandpa. You bout to have three of them running around my house and shit." Dutch joked hugging Darren and bending over to kiss Kai and his grandson on the forehead. He hugged Khloé and dapped up Elijah and Zane before he left.

Khloé, Elijah, and Zane stayed around for another hour before leaving out. Kai was happy that everyone was gone. She was beyond tired. Darren could see it, so he held baby Derrick and took a seat in the hospital rocking chair. Kai smiled looking at her boys. She took a quick picture for Instagram before falling asleep.

******

The next morning, you could feel the tension in the room. The nurse came in to check on baby Derrick and to give the results of the paternity test. Eric was also scheduled to arrive in just a few minutes. Kai could see the tension all in Darren's face.

"No matter what those results say, I still want you. You are going to have to be a father to Derrick when he's in our home. I feel it in my heart that you are his father, but the test could go either way." She said to him, her blue eyes filled with fear.

"I'm not going anywhere, swear, ma. I know he's mine, but we need to make sure your little ex understands." Darren said giving her a hug.

"Sorry to break up your little moment. Can I see my son now?" Eric walked in the room. He didn't like what he heard Kai saying. If the baby was his, there was no way he would allow some criminal like Darren to be around his son. He looked down at the baby laying inside the bassinet. He felt no connection to the baby at all. Derrick had none of Eric's family features at all. That still didn't deter him from trying to see if the baby was his.

"I got the results right here." Kai said seeing the doubt on Eric's face. She opened the folder the nurse had given her earlier and read the results out loud for everyone here. "Darren Deshawn Price is 99.9% the father of baby Derrick Price. Eric Smith has been eliminated as the potential father."

"Now you can leave the room and don't talk to my girl ever again." Darren said. He didn't give Eric any time to process what Kai had just read. The baby was his and that's all he needed to know. It was time for Eric to go. He couldn't wait to kick him out. He hoped Eric took his warning seriously and stayed away from his family. He wouldn't hesitate to body him for stepping out of line.

Eric looked to Kai and could see the relief on her face. He couldn't believe it. She actually wanted the baby to belong to this… criminal? Eric shook his head and left. This wouldn't be the last time they saw him, though.

Darren picked up Kai and kissed her all over her face causing her to giggle. He was beyond ready to take his family home. He then went over to his son and just looked at him.

He was so perfect in every way. He vowed then to always protect and love him. He had missed out on the first few years of the twins' lives and would do everything in his power to not miss out on any of Derrick's milestones.

******

It was two days after the birth of baby Derrick and Kai was more than ready to go home. The hospital bed wasn't uncomfortable, and she missed sleeping in her own bed. She was also missing the twins. They weren't her kids, but she'd always treated them like they were. She smiled at the fact that she would be going home with Darren for good. Now that it was confirmed the baby was his, they now had no concerns. She just hoped Eric stayed in his place. He hadn't tried to contact her since he left the hospital the other day, and she was glad for it.

"I got a surprise for you. Get ready." Darren said to her. He had spent the last two days out perfecting the surprise and couldn't wait to see the look on her face when she saw it.

"A surprise?" Kai said with a big smile. She loved his surprises. The last surprise Darren had got for her was her very own dance studio which was doing very well. She had a great staff that ran everything just like she were there every day.

"Yeah. Now bring your spoiled ass on." He said and smacked her on her ass. Her body was banging before, but ever since she'd gotten pregnant, her ass was on a whole other level. He couldn't wait until the six weeks was up. He was ready to slide between her legs.

"Stop." Kai giggled. She could see the lust all in his eyes. She got dressed in the Juicy sweat suit that Darren had brought for her to change into just as the nurse came in with their discharge papers.

Thirty minutes later, they were riding North on 400 past Buckhead. Kai was confused. They weren't going towards their house. She was ready to finally lay down in their bed snuggled up with her man and the twins. She was not in the mood for any stops right now.

"Where we going?" She turned and asked Darren who just smiled at her. He knew she was impatient, but she was going to love the surprise.

They took the exit and drove down a long street with million dollar mansions lining both sides of the streets. This was a very exclusive area of Buckhead with only 10 houses being sold here in the last 5 years. Kai looked at Darren again and wondered what they were doing over here. She got her answer when Darren pulled into the driveway of a huge home. Khloé and the twins were standing out front with a sign that read: "Welcome Home Kai and baby Derrick".

"Shut up!" Kai screamed as she excitedly climbed out of the passenger side leaving Darren to get baby Derrick out the back seat.

The seven thousand square foot home sat on 2 acres of land. It had 6 bedrooms, 6 full bathrooms, and 2 half bathrooms. The basement was fully finished with a media room, play room for the kids, and a man cave for Darren. Out back was a huge pool and full basketball court. Kai ran from room to room and noticed most of it was already furnished. Darren had done a wonderful job picking out the décor.

Khloé and Darren stood in the middle of the very large open concept living room watching Kai go room to room squealing in excitement. It was even funnier because the twins were right behind her. Khloé was happy for her twin. She deserved all this and more. Darren was happy he could put a smile on her face like that. He never wanted to see her hurt or be without her again.

"Well, *bro.* I'm about to head out. Thanks for making my sister happy." Khloé hugged Darren and left out of the front door.

Darren went and locked the door behind her before carrying the baby upstairs to lay him down. His family was finally together under one roof and he couldn't be happier.

Chapter 31

Jazzy stood nervously looking at herself in the full length hall mirror behind her front door. Ivy had perfectly straightened her hair then curled it to perfection. Her face was beat and her outfit was on point. She had gone with Kai to the sex shop and purchased an all lace cat-suit that left little to the imagination.

Zane would be arriving soon and she wasn't sure what his reaction was going to be. She had done everything Kai told her to do. She had cooked his favorite meal of lasagna and fried chicken wings. She purchased some body oils to give him a massage after dinner, and she was hoping to become dessert. She heard keys on the other side of the door, so she stood back and tried to strike a sexy pose.

"Babe!" Zane called out as he walked in the door with Elijah behind him.

"What the fuck!" Elijah said as he tried and failed not to take in Jazzy's body.

"Oh my God!" Jazzy said as she ran to her room to find something to cover her naked body.

"Well, I'll hit you up later." Elijah said dapping up Zane. "Make sure handle that."

"Shut up, nigga." Zane said closing the door behind Elijah. He took a deep breath before going in the room after Jazzy.

Jazzy had thrown one of his shirts on over her barely there outfit and was sitting with her back against the headboard. She was hugging a pillow and looking down, trying to hide her embarrassment. Her perfect night had been ruined, by dumbass Elijah.

"Babe." Zane said gently as he sat on the bed in front of her. "What's all this for?" He gestured with his hands at the candles and tray with oils.

"I wanted us to have a special night, but it's ruined now. You can go home." Jazzy pouted. She just knew that this was going to be the night she finally went all the way with Zane. She never thought about anyone else coming home with him, because it'd never happened before. She hadn't realized how close he had become with the boys over the last few months.

"It's not ruined, baby. Tell me what you had planned." He pulled her onto her feet and began pulling his t-shirt off her body.

"No, I can't now. The moment is over." Jazzy shook her head.

"Talk to me." Zane made a sad face that caused her to smile. "There you go. Now tell your man what's up?"

"My man?" Jazzy looked shocked at him using those words. They'd been kicking it since the night of Kai's disappearance, but hadn't put a label on anything yet. She hadn't wanted to ask because she didn't want to scare him away. Now here he was calling himself her man.

"Yeah. What you thought this was?" Zane asked confused by the shocked look on her face. He had practically moved in with her and she didn't think this was official. Girls were bogus as hell. Always needing confirmation on shit. He ate here, slept here, paid bills here, and had most of his shit here, what did she think this was?

"I don't know." Jazzy admitted feeling embarrassed.

Zane shook his head. He had been claiming her since the night after Kai's kidnapping, and she didn't even know it. He never felt the need to put a label on it because he figured everything was going perfectly. He hadn't smashed yet because he thought it would be insensitive while her friend was missing. Jazzy never really made a move on him like she was interested either. He thought she might be a virgin or something. The way she was dressed now and with edible body oils on the bed proved him wrong.

"I just—" Zane cut her off with a kiss on the lips. Laying her back he started to tear the lace of the cat-suit. He wasn't even going to try and figure out how she got that shit on. It looked like it was painted on her body. Never breaking the kiss, he started to undo his pants.

Jazzy was moaning into the kiss. They had made out before, but this was different. There was so much passion in the kiss it took her breath away. She tried to get up to help him take off her clothes. There was a zipper on the back, but he put his weight back on her pressing her down. She gave up fighting as she felt the lace being torn from her body.

Zane was finally able to tear enough of the lace off to gain access to her love box. He used his hand and began playing in her wetness. She was soaking wet down there, he couldn't wait to feel inside her. He stood up and grabbed his pants. Reaching into his pocket, he grabbed a condom and tore open the foil packet. He rolled it over his growing members. Jazzy's eyes grew wide at the sight of it. Zane had the nerve to have length and thickness.

Zane removed his shirt before stretching out over Jazzy and entering her in one swift motion.

"Fuck!" She cried out at his intrusion.

"Damn!" He said. Jazzy had some good pussy. It gripped his dick like a vice and he could hear how wet she was with each stroke. He could barely feel the condom because of how wet she was. He could die in the pussy tonight and be very happy.

"Oooh! Right there! That's my spot!" Jazzy called out as Zane found her spot. He began stroking her spot relentlessly causing her juices to pour out even more. The bed was most likely soaked underneath her.

Ten minutes later, Zane started feeling the familiar tingling of his nut rising. Jazzy's pussy was grabbing onto him so he could tell she was near her climax as well. He began giving her more deliberate strokes, wanting her to come before or at the same time as him.

"Ahhhh!" Jazzy shouted as she squirted everywhere from Zane continuously pounding in on her spot.

"Fuckkkkk!" Zane came right after her. He had never been with a squirter before and that shit was sexy as hell to him. He rolled over and lay next to her with the condom still on.

The room was silent for a minute before they both broke out in laughter. Neither one knowing why they had really waited so long to take it there. Zane was the first to gather the strength to get up. He went in the bathroom and flushed the condom. After cleaning himself off, he went back in the room with a warm towel to wash Jazzy off as well.

"Thanks, babe." Jazzy said still breathing hard.

Just then the smoke alarm began going off causing both of them to run out into the living room. Jazzy had forgot all about her lasagna in the oven and it had burned causing the room to fill up with smoke. Zane pulled the hot dish out the oven while Jazzy went and opened the doors to the patio to let the smoke out.

"And a nigga was hungry too." Zane said disappointed he wouldn't get to eat.

"Let's just order a pizza." Jazzy suggested. "There's some wings over there as well."

"Nah, it's cool, shawty. I got something else I'd like to eat." He said giving her a knowing look. Jazzy squealed with excitement as he chased her in the bedroom where they made love for the rest of the night.

******

Zane couldn't believe this day had finally arrived. For the last 7 years he had spent all his free time searching for this woman and here he was sitting in a restaurant waiting on her. He had heard so much about her that he couldn't even believe this was real. His grandma had told him so many stories about his mother before she had died, it kind of felt like he knew her already. He had so many unanswered questions to ask her.

"Oh my word!" A woman shouted. She stood next to the booth looking down at him. "You look so much like your father. But I can see me in you too."

Zane stood and hugged her. He could feel her body begin to shake as she cried. He could tell that this was just as emotional for her as well. He was glad she wasn't angry at him for tracking her down. There was just so much he wanted to know. She had just disappeared somewhere around his 4th birthday without a word and never came back. After being tossed around in foster homes for a while, he had finally met his maternal grandmother and was able to move with her. Unfortunately she died shortly after sending him back into the system.

Zarah Washington stood 5'6 with high yellow skin. She had a slim body and looked like she worked out regularly. She had brown eyes surrounded by long natural lashes. She had a cute button nose that matched his own and pink lips. He could see a lot of himself in her features which only made his excitement about their meeting grow.

"Tell me everything about you." She said breaking the staring contest they were having.

"Not much to tell, I'm a private investigator. I live with my girlfriend Jazzy. She's an assistant to a rapper." He said not going into much detail. He wasn't sure if she was really interested in his life or if she was being polite. He wanted to know more about her anyways. There'd be plenty of time to talk about himself if they decided to form a relationship.

"Well as you probably know Mr. Investigator, I just moved back to the country after living in Japan for 5 years. I spent the last 15 years traveling the world." Zarah went on to talk about her travels and different experiences. Zane hung on to her every word. A part of him was hoping she'd been through some hard times like he had, but she had simply been around the world and back not bothering to worry about her only child. Or at least he thought he was her only child.

"Do you have any other kids?" Zane asked her not sure of how he wanted her to respond.

"Oh no. You were my only one. My precious baby boy." Zarah said her eyes sparkling.

"Why did you just leave me?" Zane blurted out asking the question that had been going through his mind since she first walked in.

"I felt like your father and his family could care for you better. I was young when I had you. I wasn't ready to be a mother." Zarah explained.

"But you didn't leave me with him. I was in foster care for years before Nana came to get me." Zane was growing angry. Zarah was acting as if she left him and he had the best childhood.

Zarah was confused by the anger in Zane's voice. She had no idea what he'd been through. She had dropped him off with his father's wife when he was a little boy. She had promised that they would take care of him, and she would raise him as her own. Looking into Zane's eyes she could see the pain and anger behind them. If she'd known his life was going to turn out this way, she would have taken him with her or come back for him.

"Who is my father?" Zane asked. He had done a lot of digging but no name was on his birth certificate. His Nana never gave him any details. She refused to talk about him only referring to him as a "hoodlum" and a "thug".

"When I was younger I lived a different life. I was running with some girls who only wanted to attract men in the fast life. I have no idea how to contact him these days, but your father's name is Deshawn Price. He goes by Dutch on the streets."

Chapter 32

Darren looked in as Kai, the twins, and baby Derrick slept across their huge king-sized bed. It warmed his heart looking at his new family safe and sound laying all together. He was happy to put all the drama behind him. For the last few months things had been very quiet. With the exception of Khloé and Elijah's usual drama things were looking up for everybody. He had hoped his bro could get it together and win his girl back, but Khloé wasn't having it.

Thinking about everything that had transpired in the last year dealing with his release from prison, Camryn disappearing, and Kai's kidnapping, he held no regrets. He'd do anything to protect his family and keep them safe. Ever since he'd been locked up, all he wanted was to be able to come home to his wife and kids. Originally, he thought he'd be settling down with Camryn, but life had a funny way of giving you what you need and not what you want.

There was no doubt in his mind that Kai was the woman for him. She had found her way back to him after their short break up and that's all that mattered. She loved his children as if they were her own. She had stepped out of the spotlight with modeling jobs, but had been doing very well with her business at the studio. She was everything he could want and more.

He walked over to the bed and one by one carried each twin to their beds. It was a fight, but he finally had them sleeping in separate rooms. He kissed each one on the forehead before exiting their rooms making sure to leave their doors cracked open. He went back into the master bedroom and picked up his newest edition and placed him in the bassinet next to the bed. He didn't want to disturb Kai because she looked so peaceful, but this couldn't wait any longer.

"Kai, babe." He spoke softly, placing small kisses on her lips and neck. "Wake yo' ass up."

Kai groaned in her sleep. She had been sleeping so well. She had finally gotten everyone to settle down and wanted to get in a good nap before all the kids woke up. She tried to push Darren off of her, but he wouldn't budge. Instead, he bit into her neck and sucked gently, most likely creating a passion mark.

"Stop." She whined.

"I want to talk to you about something." Darren said lifting up her shirt and kissing her stomach. Even though she'd just had the baby 3 weeks ago and hadn't lost much of the baby weight, her body couldn't be more beautiful to him. He couldn't wait to pop more babies in her. But only after she agreed to be his wife.

"What?" She said looking down at him.

"Let's go get married." He said seriously, looking her directly in the eyes.

"What? That's your proposal?" Kai was not impressed. It was nothing like what she had imagined. She should be wearing an expensive dress and heels. Darren should have bought out an entire restaurant and filled the place with candles and flowers. Ed Sheeran would be in the background singing "Thinking Out Loud". Darren would get down on one knee and say something heartfelt and meaningful.

"You think someone else going to want you after my big head son done wrecked that shit down there?" He laughed snapping her from her thoughts. "Let's hop a plane to Vegas and make it official."

"You're so stupid." Kai smiled extra big. It wasn't some big extravagant proposal like she imagined, but she wanted nothing more than to marry him and become Mrs. Darren Price.

Taking that as a yes, he reached in his pocket and pulled out the 5 carat diamond engagement ring he'd been carrying around since they bought the baby home from the hospital. Kai's eyes began to tear up, the ring was perfect.

"Oh my God. You're serious?" She asked again as he placed the ring on her finger.

Darren didn't answer. He kissed her passionately on the lips and slid his hand down the front of her leggings until his fingers found her sex. He dipped the tip of his finger inside her love tunnel getting it wet before using it to make small circles on her already swollen clit.

"Mmmm. Damn, bae, you know we can't go there." Kai moaned. It had only been three weeks since Kai had given birth and the doctor hadn't cleared her for sex yet.

"I just want to taste it." He said moving down her body pulling her leggings off at the same time. Just as he was about to dive in, the doorbell began to ring non-stop causing baby Derrick to cry.

"I'll get him, go get the door." Kai said in a frustrated tone. She pulled up her pants and went to go see about the baby.

Darren got up, adjusted himself, and walked out of their bedroom. He was pissed that he got interrupted. Whoever was at the door kept laying on the doorbell causing a racket through the entire house.

"Yo, what the fuck is your problem?" He shouted opening the door.

"Hey, Darren." She said with a smile.

The last person he expected to see was standing in his doorway looking good as hell. The last time he'd seen her she was high out of her mind pretending to want him back. Now she was standing on his doorstep smiling like shit was sweet. He twisted his face up at her. How the fuck she even knew where he lived, he didn't know.

"Camryn…"

TO BE CONTINUED….

Text Shan to 22828 to stay up to date with new releases, sneak peeks, contest, and more…

Check your spam if you don't receive an email thanking you for signing up.